Gone Cursing

A HEX ON ME MYSTERY
BOOK SIX

KENNEDY LAYNE

GONE CURSING

DEDICATION

Jeffrey—I love the snow, but I'm not so sure about ice fishing!

Cole—You are always up for an exciting adventure, so I'll let you take my spot on the ice fishing expedition!

It's a bait and switch whodunit in the next installment of the Hex on Me Mysteries by USA Today Bestselling Author Kennedy Layne…

Creating beautiful snow angels, cross-country skiing for miles, and riding toboggans over snowy hills are all exciting outdoor activities to do in the winter months. When Lou's latest premonition of murder takes her and the gang to an isolated ice fishing shack in the middle of a lake in the upper peninsula of Michigan, it looks as if they're about to go fishing for a murderer.

You'll want to bring along a seat warmer and an ice fishing pole for this mystery if you want to help Lou and the gang hook a whale of a killer!

Chapter One

WALKING AROUND THE quaint township of Pikeville, located in the Upper Peninsula of Michigan, was like strolling through an animated version of a holiday village collection. Layers of snow lined the rooftops of old-style, heavy-built structures, while plentiful icicles hung down from the steep roofs at all different lengths. Pine wreaths and lighted candles adorned practically every window as dusk had begun to settle over the small village that was a remembrance of a simpler time when neighbors could depend on one another.

The narrow roads had been cleared of snow as best as possible, nearly hiding some of the driveways on our way in. Each lane was packed with various vehicles traveling to and from shelter. The old-fashioned lampposts shed a golden hue that glistened off the slick, compacted snow clinging to the sidewalks as residents and tourists alike hustled to their destinations, seeking warmth and protection from the bitter cold winds drifting in from the surrounding lakes. One would have thought this small village would have blown away long ago. Fortunately, it had been anchored by the dense growth of tall majestic trees.

This was the type of remote area that one could easily get lost in, and I had to admit there was quite the allure of walking into a pub that still had their string of twinkling holiday lights hung up and surrounding its entrance. Every time the door was opened by a new patron, laughter spilled out and drifted away on the gusts of icy gales.

"I'm not so sure I packed enough long johns for this case," Piper murmured through chattering teeth as she stood next to me on the curb. We were waiting for two snowmobiles to pass so that we could cross the street and enter the charming inn that even had an old-fashioned wooden sign hanging above the door. "Wait. Is that an actual trading post? I didn't even know they existed anymore."

"It sure is," I replied, scanning the other shops along the main thoroughfare of this picturesque settlement. I pulled my hat a little bit farther down to cover my cold ears, pretty sure that the falling temperatures had reached the single digits by now. "If you need to grab more thermal layers for tomorrow, we can hit the store after we check in at the front desk. We need to start canvassing the local watering holes, anyway."

"You're talking taverns and not actual fishing holes, right?"

"Right," I confirmed, leading the way across the slick road. We didn't waste time, either. Standing still for too long in this type of weather might prompt good ol' Jack Frost to make a personal visit. "But we do have to call on the collection of fishing shacks on the lake first thing in the morning, which is why you'll need those long johns."

Piper's groan was waylaid when she and I both drew up just in time to prevent a collision with two teenage boys who'd come barreling around the corner. They called out apologies, even mentioning something about how they were late for some event, but we couldn't make out their words as they took off at top speed. It was a wonder they hadn't slipped on the ice visible underneath the streetlamp.

"Did you catch what was in the blond boy's hand?" I asked, slowing my steps as we made our way to the entrance of the inn. I wish I'd been able to get a second look at what the taller boy had in his gloved hand, but I just might be able to confirm my suspicions after a small chat with the concierge. "I'm pretty sure it was a candle of some sort."

"You mean, like one for a memorial?" Piper asked, her words still managing to work their way through her chattering teeth. "I'm definitely going to need that thermal underwear sooner rather than later, aren't I?"

I didn't want to deflate Piper's hopes that we wouldn't have to walk out onto the frozen lake tomorrow. It would be the only way to speak with the witnesses who'd been in the vicinity of Ronald Dorsey's murder.

"Oh, wow," Piper exclaimed underneath her breath as we stepped inside what could only be described as a time portal. "This is beautiful. Look at the hand-carved wood surrounding the hearth. I've never seen anything like it."

The Pikeville Inn had been the only place to stay inside the village, which was where we needed to be if we were going to figure out who killed Mr. Dorsey. Technically, the place that would garner us the most information would be out on the frozen lake with the other ice fishermen, but the locals were used to tourists this time of year. Snowmobiling, ice fishing, hunting, and cross-country skiing were huge attractions around here during the winter months.

I did have to admit that there was something magical about this place. Dark cherry wooden beams were exposed throughout the main level, while the matching banister on the staircase led to a second floor with numerous doors leading to well-appointed individual rooms for the guests, as we'd seen on their website. Straight ahead of us was the intricate hearth that Piper had mentioned, where both sides of the wood had been hand-carved with a large fish jumping out of the water with its tail curled slightly for added height.

A blazing fire crackled and popped as tiny little embers could be seen floating up from the burning logs.

The flickering flames were giving off heat to a comfy sitting area that had been positioned around the inglenook for warmth. Several guests had already claimed the comfortable leather couches and chairs, enjoying drinks while carrying on what seemed to be a very deep conversation.

"No doubt that they are talking about what happened last week," I said softly so that no one would overhear me. There was no one at the front desk, which was more of a counter made from the same cherrywood as the mantled fireplace. "There's a small bell to call the attendant."

Piper and I walked up to the front desk where I tapped the silver button so that the light chime carried through the air, alerting whoever might be in the office located in a small alcove behind the counter.

I suppose now would be a great time to introduce myself.

I'm Tempest Darcinean Lilura, a descendant from the original Salem coven of witches. Yes, you definitely read that right. I'm a witch. I also have the inherent gift of telekinesis, not that it helped me much during my time of need. In my defense, I'd left my coven behind at the tender age of seventeen with the intention of living my life to the fullest without the interference of my lineage or all the baggage that was attached to it. I'd even managed to become a psychology professor at a community college in the state of Washington. My life had been full amid a wonderful career and great friends with a bright future ahead of me by my late twenties.

Everything had come crashing down around me when I had a very demoralizing run-in with the Lich Queen herself—Ammeline Letty Romilda. Basically, she was a witch who had immortalized her soul through dark necromancy magic. The name itself had become an urban legend, not that anyone in my previous community actually believed that she existed. Scary stories about Ammeline had been told at bedtime to keep little warlock boys and witch girls in check, though the storytellers had no idea that they had been reiterating ghastly truths from long ago forgotten evils.

Long story short, my encounter with the Lich Queen had ended up with me being cursed for my troubles. We're not talking a run of the mill hex, either. I'd been afflicted with visual premonitions of murders yet to come. The horrible visions I experienced were quite knee-dropping HD quality, and I'd discovered soon after that horrible experience that I just couldn't sit back and allow the people in my visions to die without trying my absolute best to prevent their deaths or at least solve their murders.

As I'm sure you've already guessed, I'm not always successful.

Hence, the reason that my friends and I were currently in the Upper Peninsula of Michigan. By the way, I go by the nickname of Lou. It definitely fit my personality a bit better than Tempest.

Piper Allifair, Orwin Cornelia, and Knox Emeric were those friends I'd mentioned who had joined me on this journey. We each had our reasons for wanting to locate Ammeline Letty Romilda and destroy her phylactery, an item which was a plain wooden cane that had the most intricate crystal handle. It was that sinister handle that now acted as the repository for her corrupted, insanely evil soul.

Aren't you forgetting someone, dear hexed one?

I looked down as I removed my gloves so that my smile wasn't visible to those around the hearth. That English-accented voice you just heard was none other than Pearl Pippa Allifair. She was a sleek and regal white feline familiar belonging to Piper, but we just referred to Pearl as our resident familiar. She'd graced the presence of many witches over her two thousand years on earth, dating back to the Cleopatra era.

Not to worry, though. Pearl had the unique ability to appear and disappear at will. From the sound of her voice, she was currently sitting on the countertop to get a better view of the room.

"Not a chance," I murmured in response. There was no forgetting Pearl and her British taste for sarcastic witticism. Orwin and Knox had stayed behind at the camping ground to secure the RV that we traveled in from mystery to mystery in between our search for Ammeline, but they should be joining us shortly. "Any problems, Pearl?"

Not in the least. As a matter of fact, Mr. Cornelia didn't even complain much about his dander allergy on the way here. He was too preoccupied with the fact that there could possibly be a UFO on the bottom of the same lake on which Mr. Dorsey met his dreadful demise while ice fishing.

Our little group had a few idiosyncrasies that might be worth mentioning, such as the fact that Orwin was a bona fide conspiracy theorist in every sense of the words. I'm talking about everything from UFOs to JFK's assassination. He was a true believer. We let his hobby slide, because he was one of the most talented warlocks who I'd ever met at such a young age of twenty-two. He also happened to be an excellent IT geek.

Now was probably a good time to bring up the fact that Knox was our resident werewolf. I'll get into more of that later. It was quite a long tale.

Quite the tale, indeed. Did you happen to mention that the two of you shared a rather intimate kiss a couple of weeks ago?

"Welcome to the Pikeville Inn. My name is Anne," a polite woman said as she made her way from the office to the counter. I gauged her age to be around twenty-three, with red hair that was naturally curly and freckles that lined the bridge of her nose. "May I help you?"

"Yes," I replied after clearing my throat. Knox and I hadn't really discussed what happened between the two of us, mostly because the kiss had taken place under a sprig of mistletoe during the recent holiday season.

Didn't that mean it was just a kiss? I had no idea, but now certainly wasn't the time to talk about it. "I have two rooms reserved under Lou Lilura for the weekend."

The fact that you're asking that question, dear hexed one, tells me that the kiss meant more to you than you're willing to admit.

While Anne pulled up our reservations on the computer, I reached into the pocket of my jacket to take out my cell phone. I had one of those cases that held my credit cards and driver's license in a small compartment on the back. Orwin had seen to it that we were able to get two rooms at the last minute.

The alien hunter does have his talents, doesn't he?

"I have you checking in this evening, checking out on Monday morning," Anne said, reading off the screen in front of her. Her attention was soon drawn to the entrance. Her eyes widened in surprise, and I didn't have to turn around to know that Knox had just walked through the door. There was no denying his magnetic appeal, with his short-cropped black hair, chiseled features, and tall, lean, muscular build. "I'll need your credit card and driver's license, please."

I handed over the two cards so that Anne could process our rooms. This was the perfect opportunity to make small talk about Mr. Dorsey's murder. The only reason I looked over my shoulder was to make sure that Orwin had accompanied Knox, but it was just our werewolf himself.

"Hey," I greeted, trying to keep things as normal as possible. We'd both been tiptoeing around the kiss underneath the mistletoe, neither one of us wanting to ruin our friendship or put a crick in our search for Ammeline. Our goals were the same, and it wouldn't be a good thing to undermine that objective at this point. "Where's Orwin?"

"He's talking to someone outside about some UFO that's supposedly at the bottom of the lake," Knox said with a confused shrug. He rubbed his five o'clock shadow, something he often did when he couldn't figure something out. "I don't get the attraction to those stories."

Mr. Emeric can join the club. Our door is wide open and accepting new membership applications.

"I'll go get him," Piper said, knowing how important it was to have Orwin by our sides when questioning someone in relation to a case. Similar to my gift of telekinesis, he had the ability to read the minds of anyone within six feet of his presence. "Give me ten seconds."

Ten seconds was long enough for me to begin nonchalantly asking what had to be on everyone's mind in this small village. I mean, someone had been murdered. Losing one of their own had to be the number one topic of conversation around these parts for the foreseeable future.

My sweet Piper has her Murder 101 app ready and

waiting to insert suspects.

"I overheard that someone died out on the lake yesterday," I said with sorrow, watching Anne closely as she checked my credit card against my driver's license. Surprisingly, she appeared a bit edgy after my question. "I'm sure with Pikeville being such a small community that you probably knew him. I'm so sorry for your loss."

"His name was Ronnie Dorsey, and he was a no-good, deadbeat husband," Anne complained, surprising all of us. It dawned on me that she reminded me of Annie Oakley. "He tempted fate and lost. It's as simple as that. You four have nothing to worry about now that Ominous Odessa has claimed herself another victim. She'll be at peace for another year, or until another fisherman does wrong by his partner."

I daresay that ill-omened perspective sent a chill down my spine. My fur has become somewhat ruffled, Miss Lilura.

Anne swiped my card through the small device, not hesitating to tell us what she believed. Most of the information we already knew, but we hadn't counted on the deep-seated belief that some of the residents seemed to have about the local urban legend. Given the fact that we'd underestimated the reality of one of the most famous supernatural folklore in history, I'm not sure why that came as such a shock.

"Who is Ominous Odessa?" I asked with skepticism, clearly feeding into Anne's desire to inform her guests on the local lore. "Are you saying that the police arrested someone?"

"Oh, no," Anne replied with a shake of her head. She tore the small piece of white paper out of the machine and laid it flat on the countertop for me to sign. "It's nothing like that. Sheriff Torkin believes it was an accident, but us locals know the truth. You see, the story of Odessa dates back to the 1800s. Legend has it that a fisherman was coming back to shore late one evening when he spotted something in the waters. He thought maybe someone had fallen off the pier, so he steered his boat closer only to find the most beautiful woman in the world treading water amongst the small waves."

Knox and I stood there listening in fascination, even though Orwin had shared with us the local myth last night over bowls of hot chili. It was one thing to hear a recounted tale from the internet, but it was another to hear it from someone who actually believed it. For being in her early twenties, Anne was a pretty good storyteller.

"Let me guess," Knox asked, getting into the creepy legend even though he already knew how it ended. He was playing his part to perfection, even altering the conclusion slightly so that it appeared we were in the dark. "The fisherman spotted a mermaid who was looking for her soulmate. I'm pretty sure that was a movie back in the eighties."

Annie took back the receipt that I'd signed and tucked it alongside the cash register. She then leaned forward on her forearms in anticipation to continue her story. It was clear that she'd done this numerous times in the past and was eager to share the rest.

"The fisherman brought his boat close enough to touch her, but she wouldn't reach for his hand. Instead, she motioned that he should get into the water with her," Annie said in almost an eerie whisper. It was quite mesmerizing. "The woman began to sing a song so alluring that he was cast under her spell. Legend has it that he dove right into the water without hesitation, joining her in the murky depths of the lake…never to be seen again."

By this time, even the group of guests near the fireplace had paused their conversation to hear the rest of the spine-chilling story. The only thing that could be heard from the other side of the room were the embers crackling as the burning firewood shifted on the metal grate.

"You see," Anne continued, lowering her voice even more so than before. "The fisherman was believed to have cheated on his wife the night before, and that he was lured to his death by a siren who supposedly haunts the dark lake waters, looking for her next victim. The villagers began to call her Ominous Odessa after the fisherman's wife. She's claimed a life almost every year since."

Well, aren't we lucky to land a murder mystery with a scorned siren swimming around underneath that thick sheet of ice? It's a good thing that we've all been on our best behavior, now isn't it?

Chapter Two

"ANNE, ARE YOU going on about that silly myth again?" a woman asked, walking down the stairs just as the front door reopened to reveal Orwin and Piper. "Please pay no attention to my daughter's silly nonsense. She thinks the tourists enjoy those old legends. She lacks any sense of propriety. I'm Anne's mother, Cecelia Dahl. Welcome to the Pikeville Inn."

Oh, my. For a moment there, I thought Mr. Cornelia might have laced my spot of warm cream with a bit of catnip. There is certainly no mistaking that these two are mother and daughter.

Pearl wasn't exaggerating, either. Cecelia might be in her late forties or early fifties, but one would never have guessed such a number if not for the look in her eyes. She and Anne could have easily passed for twins with their red curls and numerous freckles.

"I've already checked in our guests, Mom," Anne said with a grin, not appearing chagrined in the least. "All we have to do is see them to their rooms and make sure they have everything they need."

"I'm about to head out to the gathering at the wharf, so I'll let you finish accommodating our guests," Cecelia countered as she continued around the reception desk toward the office. She did level me with a knowing stare, though. "Anne gets carried away sometimes. You'll have to excuse her. She thinks those old wives' tales help business, regardless of the fact that we're usually booked year-round. You and your friends are fortunate we had a last-minute cancellation or else you'd be staying over thirty miles away from here in some sterile hotel."

I quickly glanced at Orwin to monitor his expression. He was staring at Anne with what could only be called confusion. He wasn't close enough to Cecelia to read her thoughts quite yet, but at least he wasn't waving the red flag that Anne was the guilty party.

The alien hunter seems to be taken aback by Miss Anne's belief that Ominous Odessa is real. Considering we're dealing with our own urban legend come to life from the stories around the campfire, it is something that we might want to consider—not that my sweet Piper's app handles the supernatural elements all that well.

I couldn't disagree with Pearl's assessment of the situation, but I wasn't so sure that alluring sirens actually existed. I know, I know. I'm a witch surrounded by another witch, a warlock, a talking familiar, and a werewolf. Two of being hexed by an immortal creature of legend who we were currently hunting. You'd think I'd have more of an open mind about this stuff, but sirens seemed to be a bit of a stretch.

"I was wondering why everyone seemed to be carrying candles around with them," I said, reaching a bit with another open probe. Even Piper raised an eyebrow at my comment. The only ones we'd seen with candles had been the two teenagers running down the sidewalk. Still, the far-fetched observation allowed for us to continue with the conversation. "You must be a very close-knit community to hold a vigil for a drowned fisherman."

Anne mumbled under her breath that Ronald Dorsey didn't deserve any such honor, but I focused more on Cecelia. She was currently putting on a really thick winter jacket in the doorway of her office while frowning at her daughter.

"Most of our families have been rooted here for many generations. This village is our ancestral home." Cecelia reached into one pocket and pulled out a black knitted cap, which she then proceeded to pull over the abundance of red curls. "You folks don't need to worry, though. The regularly scheduled festivities will still continue. Are you here for the ice sculpture contest, the ice fishing competition, or the polar bear plunge? I hear that the proceeds from each event this year will be going to help Esther renovate the animal shelter."

"The polar bear plunge," Knox offered up without missing a beat. He gave his most charming smile while the rest of us looked on in horror. "We usually choose a spectacular challenge each year and make it into a vacation of sorts. It keeps things exciting."

Cecelia nodded her understanding, while the rest of us tried to comprehend why Knox had chosen the worst event out of the three. I was thinking ice sculpture. I'd read an article recently where someone taped a banana to a wall, only to have it valued at one hundred and twenty thousand dollars before someone ate it. If that's the case, my intentions would have been to do absolutely nothing to the block of ice. It would have simply been titled "Unlimited Potential".

Unfortunately, Knox had to go and ruin my ingenious fabrication. He also seemed to be getting too much pleasure out of our surprise.

It's alright, dear hexed one. We'll simply have to solve this murder mystery before you and my sweet Piper end up paying the price for Mr. Emeric's poor life choices. On the bright side, this could be the alien hunter's chance for locating one of those infamous UFOs at the bottom of the lake.

"You go on ahead, Mom. I'll stay behind and make the sacrifice." Anne grabbed two sets of keys for both rooms and came around the desk. "Follow me, please. Mom is right, though. It's amazing that you were able to get two rooms on such short notice. Scott Pearson and his buddies had to postpone their arrival for the ice fishing contest until Monday. They always like to arrive early to scope out the competition first, but now they'll be arriving in town just in time to get their shanties set up."

I've always found humor in the word shanty. Odd, but quaint. I do find it quite peculiar that a fisherman would have come up with such a name. Unless, of course, he'd been trolleyed.

I could only assume that trolley was British slang for absurdly drunk. My vocabulary had certainly grown since meeting Pearl.

I hope that extends to the etiquette lessons, as well. It's very important in proper society, you know.

It was hard to miss Piper and Orwin exchange knowing stares at Anne's explanation of why we'd been able to make reservations on such late notice. You might recall that I'd mentioned Orwin's hacking skills. Let's just say he'd put them to good use, but never fear. We would never spoil Mr. Pearson's annual ice fishing adventure with his friends. They'd be here for the start of the competition, and hopefully we'd be on our way with another murder solved while attempting to find a lead on Ammeline's whereabouts.

And where did this itsy-bitsy morsel of optimism come from, dear hexed one?

"Well, the polar plunge is scheduled for Sunday morning," Anne said, keeping the conversation flowing as she led us up the grand staircase. I ignored Pearl's witticism regarding my outlook on life. You'd be a bit resentful if you'd been cursed, too. "You have tonight and tomorrow to take in what little our quaint town has to offer. The pub is having karaoke around nine o'clock tonight. If you're not into singing, the ice rink near the wharf is always a fun thing to do on a Friday night."

"Knox here loves to sing karaoke," I offered up with a bright smile, not feeling the slightest bit guilty. "We'll head on over to the pub once we get settled in."

Touché, Miss Lilura. Very well done.

Settled meant for Knox and Orwin to walk back to our two vehicles and grab our backpacks. We usually traveled light, and we most always stayed in the RV when we had the chance. Not this time around, though. Murders that took place in small towns such as this one tended to be solved through inserting ourselves into the townsfolk's lives. That meant we had to be among them, yet invisible, while the residents and tourists were going about their daily activities. How better to do that than to become tourists passing through their little town?

Anne unlocked one of the doors before handing each of the men a key to their room. She did the same with Piper and I, all the while her gaze being drawn to one of the rooms down the hall. Before I could ask her if everything was alright, Knox and Orwin claimed they'd be back with our bags.

Anne fell into step behind them, animatedly listing places that we should visit tomorrow. I was very interested in the area where we could rent snowmobiles. It would certainly make it much easier to reach the shanty where Ronald Dorsey had met his demise.

"It's a good thing you don't snore," Piper murmured, not taking long to look around the small room that would serve as our bedroom for the next two nights. There wasn't much space between the beds, nor was there much space between the end of the beds and the far wall. The room was longer in length though, allowing for a small hand-carved table with two chairs. Still, we'd definitely be tripping over one another during our stay. "I kind of like it. The room may be small, but they decorated it in such a way that it makes a person want to stay."

Pearl suddenly materialized on the bed closest to the door, her startling green eyes taking in the room as if she was a drill sergeant doing an inspection on her troops. There wasn't a smidge of dirt on her pristine white fur. She was a big proponent of keeping things orderly, which was where Piper had learned her organizational skills. With a slight movement of her front paw, she began to knead the cream-colored fuzzy blanket that had been draped over the corner of the comforter.

Oh, my! This is quite nice. Hmmm. I daresay it's the plushest material I've ever had the pleasure of kneading.

"Don't go getting sleepy now," Piper warned, knowing just how much Pearl loved her twenty-minutes naps. "We have work to do."

"Speaking of which, we really need to figure out a way to speak with Ronald Dorsey's widow." I held up a hand when Pearl would have gone into a lecture about giving an individual time to grieve over the loss of a loved one, but we were on a tight schedule that afforded us limited time. "Ronald Dorsey's funeral was yesterday, Pearl. A memorial is being held tonight, possibly because the weather cleared up a bit or the fact that it's a Friday night and opportunity struck. Either way, Anne mentioned that the police have ruled Mr. Dorsey's murder as an accident. We know different."

That's certainly an understatement, dear hexed one. Your premonition was rather graphic. The dark silhouette came right into that shanty and hit Mr. Dorsey before stuffing his body through the very hole he'd cut out for ice fishing. The suspect crammed him right down into the dark freezing water without any hesitation. I can't understand why the police would believe he simply fell into the hole. He must have had one very large contusion from the bludgeoning he took, regardless that the man's blood alcohol level was well over the legal limit. Shame on the coroner for not looking deeper.

Pearl was a bit of a control freak, so there was no doubt in my mind that she would never have more than one drink in an evening had she been human. As it stood, she was very careful with how much catnip she consumed in one setting. However, her addiction to cream was another matter altogether.

Piper and I didn't bother to shed our winter jackets. We waited patiently for Knox and Orwin to make their way back with our bags, talking over our strategy. We decided that it was best to start with the rumor of Ronald Dorsey stepping out on his wife. In order to figure out if there was any truth to that gossip, we would really need to speak with Ronald's best friend—Wallace Turnhill.

"Here you go," Orwin announced after a quick knock on our door. We'd intentionally left it ajar so that he knew that it was okay to enter. He set our backpacks down on the same bed that Pearl occupied, having already kneaded practically every part of the throw blanket. "Hey, Anne actually believes that Ominous Odessa swims the lake looking for lives to claim. So much so that she hasn't swam in the lake since she was a kid."

I highly doubt that a siren would be swimming around under five inches of ice when she could be in the warm saltwaters of Aruba this time of year. At least we can cross one resident off our suspect list, though.

"Only fifty-three to go, not including the tourists, of course," Orwin replied, apparently on board with Pearl's assessment of the siren. "We could take another twenty off that list if you were certain a woman killed Ronald Dorsey. His wife does have double motive—he was insured and there were rumors that he was quite the philanderer."

"I can't say for sure that it was a woman." All I could make out from my premonition was that the person had come up behind Ronald, hit him in the head, and shoved him into the hole. I couldn't suppress my shiver at such a horrific way to die. "Pearl?"

The way these people dress, they all look like abominable snowmen in the dark. We actually might want to put him down as a suspect. Siren, Abominable Snowman, and the list goes on.

"Well, let's see if we can't locate Ronald Dorsey's best pal," I suggested, getting a little claustrophobic. Three people and a cat were a bit much for this particular room to hold. "I'm sure Wallace Turnhill is at the memorial, but maybe he'll stop at the pub afterward to drown his sorrows. Sorry for the bad pun."

All I'm saying is that the local watering hole better have a spot of warm cream you can sneak me. We need to make this investigation pan out to make leaving this blanket behind worthwhile. Who knew it was possible to fall in love with an inanimate object so quickly?

Chapter Three

THE WATERHOLE, WHICH seemed aptly named in my opinion, was only half-full. The fact that everyone seemed to be at the memorial for Ronald Dorsey allowed us the ability to choose a booth with a clear view of the front entrance. The lively place was just as one would picture a pub in such a quaint village. It actually resembled something out of the Wild West in the winter, with everything covered in roughhewn wood planks...even the walls.

What is the appealing nature of tossing peanut shells on the ground? Simply repulsive behavior, if you ask me.

Pearl was once again invisible as we settled into the booth, although she was a bit on the irritable side after being forced to leave the blanket back at the inn. Knox and I were both a bit wary when it came to exposing our backs in public, so we sat together on one side up against the wall so that we could both keep an eye on the people spilling in from the cold.

"Reception is spotty in this area, but I was able to use the inn's Wi-Fi before we left to pull up Wallace's picture." Orwin slid his phone into the middle of the table, allowing all of us to get a good look at the man who resembled an unkept lumberjack. "He's fifty-six years old, single, and owns the bait and tackle store near the wharf."

"That's quite the beard," Piper commented on the picture. She scrunched her nose, and I already figured out what thought had crossed her mind. "Do you think he brushes it at least once a week? I'm pretty sure those are crumbs."

You'll be interested to know that a lot goes into the upkeep of such facial hair. Did you know that—

"Scoot," I directed Knox, not wanting to be a part of this conversion. Pearl was a walking encyclopedia when it came to almost everything to do with anything. Apparently, facial hair was included on that list. I wasn't necessarily opposed to beards, especially upon recalling my kiss with Knox underneath the mistletoe. Granted, his was more of a five o'clock shadow, but this particular topic was bringing up memories that were best left alone. "I'll go grab us some drinks."

"I'll go with you," Knox replied, causing me to wonder if he was thinking of our intimate exchange, as well. We both walked the short distance to the bar, catching the attention of the same man featured in the painting hung on the back wall. He must be the owner. "Could we get four regular draft beers, please? Whatever you have on tap is fine."

"Coming right up," the man replied, his voice deeper than I would have guessed. He had the type of features that made it hard to tell his age, but I still estimated him to be in his sixties. "Let me guess. You're in town for the polar bear plunge. Esther is going to be mighty pleased with such a good turnout this year. Those folks in the back came all the way up from Arizona, if you can believe that. You young'uns are something else. No amount of money could get me in that cold water this time of year. I'm Trout, by the way, spelled the same as the fish."

Knox gave a very satisfied smile that he'd chosen the one activity that the townsfolk would believe we'd come to partake in, though I still thought we appeared artistic enough to join in on the ice sculpture competition. Still, the conversation gave us an opening to ask questions. What I really wanted to know was if the bartender had really been named after a fish, but I started off slow.

"We saw all the shanties on the ice," I said, reaching into the bucket of peanuts to give myself something to do while we waited for our drinks. "Where does the town host the polar bear plunge if the entire lake is frozen? Are they cutting open a big hole?"

"On the opposite side of the lake is an area that doesn't freeze. They have several pumps there that circulate the water and aerate it to maintain the oxygen level in the lake," Trout replied, tilting the glass as he filled one of the glasses with draft beer. He timed it perfectly so that a half-inch thin layer of foam formed and floated near the rim of the mug. "There will be snowmobiles available to pull the participants across the ice on large tubes. Don't you worry none. Henry has you covered."

I wasn't sure who Henry was, but it looked as if we'd find out, provided that we were still around on Sunday. It didn't take me long to crack the peanut. I decided to set the split shell next to the tin bucket to appease Pearl, who was probably still back at the table explaining the proper way for a man to take care of his beard.

"With all the festivities planned this weekend, I expected this place to be hopping," Knox said, taking the first draft beer and sliding it my way. I nodded my approval at the tactic of bringing up the memorial. "We're staying over at the inn, and it's pretty quiet there, too."

"That's because the villagers are holding a memorial for Ronald Dorsey. Poor chap," Trout murmured with a solemn shake of his head. He filled a second mug. "One of our own had an accident earlier this week. He fell into the water and couldn't get back out. Shame, really. He shouldn't have been out on the ice so late at night by himself. He knew better, but that doesn't give the family comfort. Anyway, this place will be packed with locals fairly soon."

"We're sorry to hear that," Knox replied, taking the second beer. I cracked another peanut. "I'm glad to hear that it was an accident, though. We thought we overheard someone say at the inn that the man had been murdered. You can imagine we were a bit wary hearing that first thing upon checking in."

I was pretty impressed with the way that Knox was handling this so-called interview. I popped another peanut in my mouth, almost choking on it when Pearl made one of her infamous "I'm still invisible but dropping in on your conversation" right out of the blue visits. From the sound of her English-accented voice, she'd chosen to sit on top of the bar versus the floor.

I'm not getting that spot of warm cream this evening, am I?

Knox lifted an eyebrow at my coughing fit, and I shrugged off his attempt of dislodging the peanut. I'd finally gotten myself under control when Trout had to go and cause me to quickly inhale the peanut once again. The benefit of me being a witch was my ability of telekinesis. I shifted slightly away and was able to dislodge the little nuisance without anyone the wiser.

You certainly are having trouble maintaining your composure this evening, dear hexed one. Maybe you should lay off those peanuts, hmm?

"It wouldn't surprise me at all to find out that Marilyn murdered Ronnie after hearing the rumors that have been flying around lately," Trout proclaimed, finishing up the two remaining mugs of beer and setting them both down in front of Knox. "I don't like to speak ill of the dead, but that woman deserved better than a man like him. He was always searching for ways to take a shortcut. That doesn't mean he should have died in such a heinous manner, though."

I held up my hand to let them know that I was okay, even though my eyes were now watering profusely. Trout thankfully handed me a cocktail napkin.

"Karma, if you ask me," a man at the bar announced unbidden.

I do so love meeting people with the same mindset. This gentleman has given me incentive to go visit the other patrons. I realize that the probability is almost nil, but I will take the chance of retrieving myself a spot of warm cream if the chance arises. I'd be forever in your debt.

"That's Hank," Trout introduced, tossing a bar towel over his shoulder. "Don't mind him. He doesn't like anyone or anything."

"Maybe if you hadn't taken the boiled eggs off the menu, people would be a bit nicer to you," Hank grumbled, the color of his eyes a rather startling blue for someone of his age. They were trained on us, though. "If one can't be faithful to a woman as beautiful as Marilyn, then Lady Karma will step in...and rightfully so. Hey, I don't imagine the two of you ice fish, do you? I've got a shanty I need to rent out, and I don't have any takers."

I let Knox explain how we were in town for the polar bear plunge while I glanced over my shoulder in hopes that Orwin would catch the hint that he should amble over to the bar. His telepathy would certainly come in handy right about now. I didn't expect to find the booth we'd been occupying empty. I scanned the bar to find both Orwin and Piper playing darts with a group of people around the same age.

"...love to, but I've never tried ice fishing before. Do you rent by the day? I might actually take you up on that offer."

I almost got whiplash at Knox's question, shooting him a warning glance that should have spoken volumes. We didn't have time for him to take up a new sport. At least, I was pretty sure that some people considered fishing a sport. Either way, we needed to solve this murder before Sunday morning before we ended up jumping voluntarily into freezing water.

"You swing by my place at the lake, and I'll see to it that you're set up with everything you need. What's your name, young man?"

"Knox Emeric. And this is Lou Lilura." Knox leaned forward to peer around me, motioning toward Orwin and Piper. He introduced them by first name only before gathering up the three beers in his hands. "I'll see if I can't get Orwin to join me tomorrow morning. I know that Lou and Piper wanted to hit some of the small shops around town."

Knox began to lead the way back to the booth we'd occupied earlier. I could hear Hank boasting to Trout that he still had a knack for suckering in the tourists, which didn't bode well for Knox's credit card tomorrow. I slid into the booth first, careful not to spill my own draft while making room for Knox so that we could both continue to watch the front entrance. It shouldn't be long before those who attended the memorial stopped by for a drink to commemorate their friend's life.

Orwin and Piper were still finishing up their game of darts, so we sat in an awkward silence that had been shoved between us ever since we'd shared a kiss underneath the mistletoe. In my defense, I hadn't been expecting it. I'd reacted without thinking, which was easy to do when a handsome man such as Knox Emeric made a welcomed but bad-timed advance.

I mean, we had a lot on our plate. I've already shared my story, but Knox's past was just as complicated than mine, if not more so. All he'd done was gone for a healthy hike in the mountains, only to come upon a cave that Ammeline had holed up in with her phylactery performing some kind of ceremony or something. I never did have the heart to ask if she'd been dressed or sans clothes, but honestly that was an image I didn't want in my head. Anyway, she'd cursed him with a special brand of lycanthropy. That's right…she had taken an ordinary human man and turned him into a massive hairy beast capable of rendering a normal person limb from limb.

I don't want you to think that was what he looked like right now, because his appearance was quite the contrary to that. His attractiveness was the reason for my lapse of judgement underneath the mistletoe. We simply did not have time to throw in a romantic complication upon such a vital and dangerous endeavor.

"We should probably talk about it," Knox said, not even bothering to ease us into such a conversation.

"Probably not."

"You don't want to complicate things?"

"If I didn't know any better, I'd think you had switched places with Orwin."

"Orwin wasn't the one who kissed you underneath the mistletoe."

Was it hot in here? I'm pretty sure that Trout had turned up the heat when I wasn't looking. I tried to come up with why I'd decided to wear a black turtleneck, but I already knew the answer. It had fit well underneath my winter jacket.

"Fine. Let's agree to table it for another time, preferably after we've taken care of our shared Ammeline situation." Knox took another long draw of his beer, not taking his dark gaze off the front entrance. The fact that he still wanted to have a discussion after what could be months or longer in completing our mission told me that it hadn't just been a simple kiss. I lifted my own mug so that he couldn't catch a glimpse of my smile. "We'll go on in the meantime with business as usual."

"Agreed," I replied softly.

Etiquette had me not interrupting your private conversation, dear hexed one, but I daresay the attraction between the two of you could burn this quaint little tavern to the ground. Watching the two of you is just like enjoying one of those movies that Piper is fond of on the Hallmark or Lifetime channels. I can't wait to see what happens after the next commercial…in this case, our current murder mystery.

Chapter Four

"I CAN'T BELIEVE that Knox talked Orwin into going ice fishing at four o'clock in the morning. Does he have some kind of compulsion power that we don't know about?" Piper wrapped the pink scarf she'd knitted herself a week ago and looped the ends around each other so that it hung down the front of her jacket. We actually all had matching scarves, mittens, and hats in various annoyingly bright colors. Let's just say that she had gone on a knitting spree over the holidays, and she hasn't stopped since. "We didn't even get back here to the inn until after eleven."

I've just come back from checking on them, and our resident alien hunter is currently visiting all the shanties with some excuse about needing to find certain bait. I do believe he's chosen something that is rare, but it is giving him an opportunity to read everyone's thoughts. If Ronald Dorsey's killer is somewhere out on that frozen lake today, Mr. Cornelia will find him.

"It's good to know that we're fast-tracking this case," I said, having caught the slightest impression of nausea last night that I usually experience if Ammeline happens to be within a hundred-mile radius. She was close, and we needed to have the time available to hunt her down. "Let's hit the shops in town and speak with those on the suspect list we created last night."

Ronald Dorsey's best friend, Wallace, hadn't shown up at the pub last night. Those who came from the memorial were all talking about how Marilyn had lit a candle on the wharf and then simply walked back home without talking to anyone. Who could blame her? Everyone assumed that her husband was having an affair, but how much truth was there to those rumors? Wouldn't someone know who the other woman was in that scenario? Keeping a secret in this town had to be nearly an impossible feat.

One would think so, dear hexed one. With a village this small, it would be rather hard to get away with a sordid affair without someone knowing something about the other party.

"Diner," both Piper and I said in unison.

Such a place was usually a goldmine of information. The residents were probably used to eating and gossiping with one another, similar to the local watering hole, only with more of a family atmosphere. Seeing as the memorial had been held last night, it only stood to reason that the major subject of chinwag would still be Ronald Dorsey.

I'd already opened the door to our room, waiting for Piper to sling her body purse over her head and settle it on top of her jacket. I purposefully didn't carry a purse of any kind, preferring to have free use of my hands and arms in the case the need arose for me to use my ability of telekinesis.

Piper was walking toward me when she focused on someone behind me. The slight frown marring her brow told me that it wasn't anyone she recognized.

"Morning," a deep rattling voice said, causing me to turn to find a man coming out of the room that Anne had been fixated on last night. He was average height, had brownish hair that appeared darker due to the products he'd apparently used after his morning shower, and didn't seem to be a fisherman in the least. He also didn't strike me as someone who was used to the cold, either. The winter boots he was currently sporting were brand new, and I would guess the same thing for the winter coat he held in his left hand. "Have a good day, ladies."

Ah, a gentleman with manners. I do so like the clientele of this quaint little inn.

By this time, Piper had joined me on the threshold of our room. We both stepped out into the hallway and observed the man as he walked down the stairs with what appeared to be a destination in mind.

"He isn't here to fish," Piper speculated, noting the man's attire, as well. "He also doesn't strike me as the type of individual who would jump into freezing water, no matter what the cause."

I certainly wouldn't have said our neighbor across the hall was the creative type either, though he could simply have a relative in the area. It was January, so maybe he had come to visit family for the holidays and had extended his stay.

"Pearl, would you—"

I'm on it, but I'd like there to be a spot of warm cream waiting for me when I meet up with you two at the diner.

"Count on it," I replied, waiting for Piper to lock our door behind her. We made our way downstairs, but the man must have already left the inn. The only one we saw was Anne, who was behind the front desk organizing what looked to be invoices. "Good morning."

"Did you enjoy karaoke last night? I heard that Hank put on quite the show," Anne said with a big smile on her face. "I've heard that man sing before, and I'm surprised that your ears aren't still bleeding."

"We didn't stay long enough to hear him," Piper replied, tugging her knitted cap lower onto her blonde locks with a bright smile. "Everyone seems so nice here, so we thought we'd do a little bit of exploring. Knox and Orwin went ice fishing, but we were going to take in the shops today. How is the food at the diner?"

"Oh, Bev makes the best cherry cobbler," Anne raved, setting aside her pile of papers to lean forward on the counter. "You'll also want to try the biscuits and gravy that she makes for the breakfast special. They are to die for."

Had Pearl still been in attendance, I'm sure she would have had something to say about Anne's ability to throw around phrases such as those after Ronald Dorsey's death. Granted, most everyone in town believed that he had been drinking and fallen into his own fishing hole by accident. Anne believed different, though. Something told her that there was more to his death, or she wouldn't be so eager to say an urban legend had collected the man's soul for not being faithful to his wife.

"Have a good day, you two," Anne called out as she turned her focus back on the paperwork in front of her.

"Um, Anne?" I waited for her to look at us before I posed my next question. "Who is the man staying in the room across the hall from us?"

The concern that crossed her freckled features told me that the guest wasn't here visiting family. Anne and her mother probably remembered every single guest who came through the front door for the past few years or more. Granted, this could be his first year doing one of the activities planned by the village to lure in tourists, but it was clear that Anne believed differently.

"Mr. Nektar claims he's just passing through." Anne pursed her thin lips, a signal that she didn't believe the man's assertion.

"He must value his privacy," I speculated, wanting to give Anne a bit of help as she seemed to struggle with her next sentence. "Basically, you're not sure why he's in town."

"Something like that, yes."

I came from a small village myself, although the majority in my lineage referred to it as a coven. We welcomed others in with open arms and expected the same treatment in return. If Mr. Nektar came to town with an unfriendly and aloof manner, the locals wouldn't take too kindly to that. Hopefully, Pearl would be able to sniff out exactly what Mr. Nektar was doing in town. Considering that the sheriff and his department had already ruled Ronald Dorsey's death as accidental, no one would be tracking the man's movements.

I could see that Anne was looking at both Piper and I with curiosity, and I didn't want to push the issue. It was best I let the topic drop, so I flashed her a smile and told her that we'd see her later this afternoon. Piper had already opened the door, so the cold wind reached out to me before I ever crossed the threshold.

"I'm starving, so let's hit the diner before we go to the trading post for my thermal underwear. What I currently have on underneath my jeans is not going to cut it." Piper pulled her knitted cap lower over her ears as we began to walk into the wind. "How do people live in this frigid weather?"

"It's more the community and the family bonds that have been made over the centuries." We crossed the street, both of us searching for any sign of Mr. Nektar. He wasn't anywhere to be found. Hopefully, Knox and Orwin were having better luck on their fact-finding mission. "You have to admit that this is a beautiful area."

"Can't your next premonition be in Florida?" Piper quipped, although there was a trace of hope in her tone. "The beach is sounding quite nice at the moment."

"Keep thinking about the sun and the sand," I urged, attempting to stop my teeth from chattering. This type of cold wasn't the same as what was in Pennsylvania or Massachusetts, that's for sure. "Or a nice hot cup of coffee."

We'd quickened our step, passing by a few people who were out and about this morning. They were probably locals, while we were standing out like a sore thumb. Neither Piper or I cared at this point, and I found myself grateful that Knox and Orwin had been the ones to go out on the lake today in search of clues.

"In we go," Piper urged, though it sounded more like a plea as we came upon the entrance to the diner.

We were inside as quick as possible, both of us sighing with relief when we felt heat blowing on top of us from over the foyer that was activated by the door. The diner had a built-in electric heater above the entrance that had me wondering if we couldn't have something similar in the RV. It was simply miraculous.

"Welcome to the Pikeville Diner," a woman greeted with a bright smile. According to the nametag, her name was Bethany. "Just the two of you this morning?"

"Yes, please," I responded as Piper lifted her face to the blowing hot air coming out of the contraption overhead. "A booth, preferably."

We'd gotten into a great routine when making sure that Pearl got her spot of warm cream upon visiting the numerous diners that we've eaten at over the course of our trips. It wasn't like the town was huge, so Mr. Nektar should be reaching his destination soon. Once Pearl had a chance to listen in on any conversations that might be taking place, she'd be joining us rather quickly.

"Take your pick," Bethany directed, motioning toward what remaining tables and booths were available. This was clearly a first come, first serve setup. "Menus are on the table."

I led the way, weaving through the middle of the diner to reach the one booth available against the wall. I'd be able to keep an eye on the door, while being close enough to some of the tables in the middle of the diner to hear a few of the discussions taking place. It didn't take us long to remove our outerwear and make ourselves comfortable.

"Let me guess," an older woman said as she came up to the table in a pair of jeans, a long-sleeved shirt with the name of the diner on the left pocket, and a short white apron tied around her waist. "You two are here for the ice sculpture competition. I'm Bev, by the way."

I lifted my eyebrow in satisfaction toward Piper to indicate that my idea had been the most believable. She rolled her eyes and reached for the menu.

"Actually, we're here for the polar bear plunge," I

ended up saying, thanks to Knox. "We thought we'd spend the day sightseeing and shopping, though the weather is quite cold outside."

"I didn't take you two for the plunge type," Bev said, pouring me a piping hot cup of coffee. Piper had not turned over her cup, as she had every intention of ordering a cup of tea and a spot of warm cream, which usually wasn't questioned when ordered together. "Esther is having a great turnout this year. The animal shelter should be able to buy new beds for each kennel, with enough food for the next year. Good for you two for taking on such a cause."

"We were hesitant to start our trip, thinking that maybe the event would be canceled after the death of Mr. Dorsey." I took a menu myself, although I'd already decided to have the biscuits and gravy. "We're from small towns ourselves, so we know how an unexpected death of someone as prominent as Mr. Dorsey can affect the activities of a place like this."

Bev frowned, almost as if she didn't want to discuss such personal details about one of their own. Typically, that's what happened with a small town, but the majority of the tourists in this village came back every year. Most of them ended up being treated with familiarity and welcomed back with open arms.

"We heard the news from Anne," I said, hoping to bring a sense of ease to Bev's misgivings. It worked like a charm. "We're really sorry for the town's loss."

"I'm sure you've heard a lot about good ol' Ronnie, but I never had a problem with him. Rumor had it that he was stepping out on Marilyn, but those two had just had their thirty-year wedding anniversary this past spring." Bev shook her head in dismay. "Marilyn loved that man with all his faults. He was always searching for the pot of gold at the end of the rainbow, you know?"

Before I could ask any more questions, Bev was being told that an order was up at the window. She told us to take our time perusing the menu and that she would be back with the tea and spot of warm cream that Piper had asked for before Bev could leave our table.

"Well, the boys actually seem to be enjoying themselves," Piper divulged after having checked her phone for messages. She turned it toward me so that I could see a picture of a smiling Knox holding up a fish. "Orwin said that he's visited at least ten shanties so far, and everyone seems to believe that Mr. Dorsey's death was an accident. One of the younger fishermen repeated the siren tale, though. He truly believes something lurks in depths of the lake. It seems Anne isn't the only one who believes in Ominous Odessa."

Piper decided on an omelet instead of the biscuits and gravy, so we waited patiently for Bev to come back for our order while attempting to listen in on some of the other surrounding discussions. A couple who was sitting in the booth behind me were talking about their son having a chance to win the ice fishing contest this year, while two older gentlemen sitting at a table to our left were discussing the football playoffs and how the pub was planning on hosting a championship party.

"So, what'll you two have this morning?" Bev asked, coming up to the table with a pad and pen in her hands. We gave our orders, and I was able to not-so-nonchalantly bring up Ominous Odessa. The name had a few heads turning our way, especially after Bev's laughter had practically burst into shooting stars around the diner. "You have been talking with Anne Dahl, haven't you? That girl believes every urban legend ever told, from Ominous Odessa to vampires. She lives in a fairytale world."

"Little Anne might be right about Ominous Odessa, though." One of the two gentleman had decided to chime in, the topic of an old wives' tale too much to resist. "Remember that tourist last year? He fell through the ice, and his best friend swore he saw something in the water below."

"Those two amateurs had no idea how to ice fish, Wallace. They used a darn chainsaw to cut a huge honking hole into the ice. The guy who lived was lucky that he hadn't been close enough to get pulled down into the water himself." Bev shook her head in disbelief before zeroing her gaze on the man in question. "Why aren't you two out on the ice today? Ronnie would have wanted you to continue with the contest, you know."

"Doesn't seem right this year, Bev."

Piper and I exchanged a knowing look, not having expected to run into Ronald Dorsey's best friend. Pearl would have had our heads if we disrespected someone who was grieving, but we couldn't solve this murder without the help of Mr. Dorsey's friends and family. In our defense of not recognizing the bushy beard and lumberjack appearance, it was due to several diners having the same sense of style. They all even wore the same plaid shirts tucked into denim jeans and caps over their heads. It was a literal forest of lumberjacks.

I don't believe that you'll be needing to bother Mr. Wallace Turnhill during his breakfast, dear hexed one.

Piper leaned forward while I straightened in my seat. Bev, by this time, had made her way over to Wallace's table in an attempt to urge him back out onto the ice to partake in the ice fishing contest. Pearl's spot of warm cream was on the table, but hopefully Pearl would spill the goods before she settled in to enjoy her treat.

"What did you find out on your scavenger hunt?" I asked softly, my hopes rising a bit upon hearing Pearl say that we wouldn't need to question Wallace. That could only mean that she'd discovered something very juicy. "Please tell me that you were able to crack the case."

There is a good chance that Mr. Nektar should be in the number one slot of my sweet Piper's Murder 101 app. You see, Mr. Nektar works for a rather large corporation who takes small towns such as Pikeville and turn them into massive resorts that offer their guests all the modern amenities their little hearts could desire. I do believe I may have discovered the motive in this murder mystery.

Chapter Five

"SEE?" PIPER POINTED out as she browsed the women's thermal underwear section at the trading post. It was a cute building that housed quite a bit more selections of clothing than I had anticipated. "How convenient was it that Knox chose the polar bear plunge? It's exactly where we need to be, so that should be our first stop."

I pursed my lips in an effort not to say anything about the fact that Knox's choice was the worst of the three or four alternatives to us. We'd come to find out while enjoying our breakfast at the diner that Marilyn volunteered at the animal shelter. She was helping Esther organize this year's charity event.

You're missing the silver lining here, dear hexed one. My sweet Piper could have knitted you thermal underwear. Did you see the booties she knitted me? As much as I adore the kind gesture and the time she devoted to knitting them, my pristine white fur clashes with bright pink.

"I'm just saying that Marilyn could have easily been the artistic type and hosted the ice sculpture contest," I countered, losing my own battle of wills to remain silent. "Hey, did you feel this material? I might need to buy a set of these myself."

The set of thermal underwear came in black, too. Who could pass up such a bargain? I looked at the tag. The sale price was amazingly affordable.

You do realize that the store most likely raised the price, slashed it to look as if it was on sale, but in actuality you're paying the regular price needed for the owner to make their thirty to fifty percent markup on the item in question?

"Don't rain on my parade, Pearl," I muttered, figuring out that she was sitting on top of one of the several racks of clothes. "Piper, are you almost ready?"

When she didn't answer right away, I looked over my shoulder to find that she'd wandered closer to the counter. By happenstance, Hank was standing there talking to the cashier, who appeared to be in his sixties. The two seemed to be engaged in a serious conversation, and I could easily see that Piper was attempting to eavesdrop on their conversation.

No need to ask, dear hexed one. I won't be but a moment.

Now that I'd chosen my own set of thermal underwear, I began to weave my way through the racks of clothes and other items that were often found at a trading post. The clothes mostly consisted of standard items, but there was a lot of interesting material for crafts to be purchased, as well.

"I saw Hank come in after you walked toward the

back," Piper whispered, feigning interest in a floral material that someone would most likely purchase if they were making pillows or a comforter set. "He doesn't look happy."

It turned out that Pearl hadn't needed to position herself closer to the two men. Both Hank and the cashier were now in a heated argument that became rather loud over the next thirty seconds.

"…can't believe that Henry would ever consider such an offer, and I can't believe that you would, either," Hank spouted, apparently no longer caring who overheard him. "I never thought I'd see the day when a Sampson sold out the family business. Your grandfather must be rolling over in his grave right this minute."

Shame, shame, shame. That was unwarranted. One should never bring in one's lineage like that in an argument. It never bodes well, but I do believe such low depths proves our pub regular heard about Mr. Nektar's meeting with the gentleman who rents out those quaint little shanties. I would like to pay a visit to Mr. Cornelia and Mr. Emeric before the day is through.

I'm pretty sure that Pearl just wanted a chance to taste a fresh fish herself.

On the contrary, dear hexed one. I am not a heathen, unlike you with your coffee addiction. I would simply be observing from afar. I prefer my fish to be properly cooked.

"Hank, I just told the man I'd consider his offer," Mr. Sampson replied wearily, his worried gaze darting our way when he realized that we had items in hand and that we were ready to check out. "It was just to get him off my back. Now, I have customers. Why don't we bring this up at the townhall meeting next week? I think that would be the proper venue to discuss the issue."

"And what if someone gives in before then, huh?" Hank asked, not caring that tourists were hearing the town's latest chinwag. "All it takes is one of us to cave in order to cause a domino effect, and I'm not selling out our hometown for some green pieces of meaningless papers."

Hank brushed past us with a murmur of apology underneath his breath, but his honesty had laid the groundwork for that motive Pearl had discovered earlier this morning. Two theories came to mind. The first being that maybe Ronald Dorsey had been the weak link in this scenario. Maybe, just maybe, someone discovered that he was going to sell his lake property and wanted to stop him from carrying out such a hasty mercenary decision.

I take it your second theory would be Mr. Dorsey turning down Mr. Nektar's proposal and the two getting into an argument that led to Mr. Dorsey's demise? If we go with your initial theory, the suspect pool becomes the size of the lake that Mr. Cornelia and Mr. Emeric are currently fishing on. There are a lot of villagers who would not want a sale of that nature to go through, dear hexed one.

Pearl was right, but there might be someone who could clarify if Ronald Dorsey had even been tempted in the slightest to sell his lake property. There was only one way to find out, and that meant using the dressing room to layer up with these thermal underwear and head out on a fact-finding mission.

"Good morning," Mr. Sampson greeted, feigning ignorance that we'd witnessed his conversation with Hank. "Let me guess—ice sculpture contest."

I do believe that the villagers have made it a game to predict what festivities the tourists have chosen. I can see the fun in such a community sport.

"We're here for the polar bear plunge," Piper said with a smile, setting down the pink thermal underwear that she'd chosen onto the counter. "We wanted to support the efforts of the animal shelter. I have a beautiful cat myself, and I love her more than anything in the world."

My sweet Piper certainly knows how to make me verklempt, doesn't she?

Piper and Mr. Sampson began to talk about all the charities that the local festivities supported, and they both agreed that each one added value to the village. I motioned that I would pay for both items, pulling my phone and credit card from my coat pocket before utilizing the verbal opening to our advantage in solving this murder mystery.

"We couldn't help but overhear that someone is in town trying to purchase some of the lakeside property." I swiped my credit card through the machine before sliding it back into the pouch on my phone case. "It would be really sad to see this charming village turn into another sterile resort bent on greed."

"Oh, I highly doubt that it would come to that," Mr. Sampson replied with a frown, finishing up our purchases. We'd already explained that we were going to use the dressing room to put them on before going outside, so he didn't bother to put the items in a bag. "The majority of the founding families wouldn't sell out their ancestors in such a despicable way. You'll be safe planning your trip back for next year's polar bear plunge, ladies."

"We're glad to hear that, especially since we didn't think this year's planned activity was going to take place after we heard about that horrible accident out on the lake last week," I replied, taking my set of black thermal underwear from Piper. "We're staying at the inn, and there are some pretty far-out theories about what happened to that poor man. Some are even suggesting murder."

"Anne is spouting her tales about Ominous Odessa, isn't she?" Mr. Sampson said with a laugh, clearly familiar with the younger woman's obsession with the infamous urban legend. "I'm pretty sure that folklore was made up to teach young men and women that infidelity wouldn't be tolerated in this town. Marriage is sacred, and what better way to enforce that belief than to create a myth to hammer that principle home for the heathens among us?"

I'm all for the sanctity of marriage, but I'm not so sure about their method utilized to teach the young'uns such a family value.

To be honest, I was a bit surprised to hear Pearl's opinion on the matter. Her favorite word in the dictionary was *eviscerate*, much to Orwin's utter horror.

"That's not to say that Ronnie stepped out on Marilyn," Mr. Sampson quickly said, making sure that we knew his stance on the subject. "I personally don't believe that he would have done such a thing, but he was one who didn't much care what others thought. I swear that man had fun stirring up the townsfolk as if it were his favorite pastime."

"You're just defending Ronald Dorsey because he was on your sacred bowling team." The nasally voice belonged to the woman who I'd seen come into the trading post a few minutes ago. She had to be in her early seventies, but she still grabbed a pair of leather work gloves from the pile on top of a table with a sale sign sticking up from the middle of the heap. It was clear from her worn winter jacket and weathered face that she was still very active. "Wallace attempted to cover for Ronnie the day before his accident, but everyone knows that Ronnie was at Debra Lily's house that night. His vehicle was parked behind her shed most of the evening."

"Don't you go spreading rumors, Ms. Rusco," Mr. Sampson warned good-naturedly, shaking his head at us to indicate that we should take anything this older woman had to say with a grain of salt. "You know that Debra and Henry have been seeing each other for over a year. Henry and Ronnie have the same make and color of car, that's all."

I've always been fascinated with how rumors get started, though I am surprised that Ms. Rusco got her facts wrong. She doesn't strike me as the type of woman to belong to the gossip mill.

"Marilyn is my niece," Ms. Rusco exclaimed in defiance. She tilted her chin, causing her long grey braid to fall over her shoulder. "That Ronald always put money ahead of everything, and she always deserved better. I'm taking her to the diner tonight for their fish tacos. I know how important it is to keep busy at a time like this, even though she shouldn't be crying over a man who valued material items more than his family's wellbeing."

I do believe we might have another prominent suspect to type into that app of yours, my sweet Piper.

Technically, Ms. Rusco's name would have already been included in the suspect pool since everyone in town had reason to ensure that Ronald Dorsey didn't sell off his lake property. Hank was right when he said that towns like this one could have a domino effect when crumbling to the ground under the weight of a gigantic corporation making a bid for a hostile takeover of the town's future. With that said, Ms. Rusco's motive went a little deeper than most.

"Well, we should add on these layers before heading over to the animal shelter," I replied in an effort to disengage from the conversation. We still had a lot of ground to cover and a lot of people to talk to in hopes of finding a lead as to who murdered Ronald Dorsey. "We're going to register early for the polar bear plunge tomorrow morning."

Speaking of the polar bear plunge, have you come up with an excuse as to why you won't be jumping into the ice-choked water, dear hexed one? I'm relatively sure the only thing that could entice me to do such an idiotic thing is an endless supply of warm cream. In retrospect, I technically already have that at my disposal. Therefore, my answer would be a resounding no.

I still planned on solving this case by this evening and driving out of Pikeville as fast as my red Jeep could go on these icy backroads. By registering early, my donation would be put to good use.

"Dressing rooms are in the back," Mr. Sampson informed us with a pointed finger to boot. "Now, Ms. Rusco, was there a decal on the back of that car you saw? Henry has a…"

Mr. Sampson and Ms. Rusco continued to talk about her belief that Ronald Dorsey was having an affair with Debra Lily while Piper and I made our way to the dressing rooms. We waited until we were out of earshot to discuss our findings.

"I know we need to speak with Marilyn, but we should also try to figure out a way to talk with Debra," Piper suggested, holding her pink thermal underwear close to her chest, probably at the mere thought of having to walk outside again. I could only imagine how cold the guys were out on the ice. "I'll text Orwin. Now that he and Knox had all but ruled out the fishermen on the lake, they can accompany us to talk with the townsfolk."

Fantastic idea, but don't worry about texting our dear colleagues, my sweet Piper. I will go fetch them myself.

Pearl's light laughter surrounded us once she realized the pun that she'd created was once again in regard to Knox. I'm sure that he wouldn't have appreciated her sense of humor, but it was hard not to crack a smile at the way she constantly entertained herself with her dog jokes. She'd said from the very beginning of our journey that I take things too seriously and could be a bit of a pessimist. Well, it was kind of hard not to be when I was hunting down the Lich Queen in order to save what was left of my sanity. In the meantime, Pearl somehow thought knock-knock jokes were the way to ease my tension.

In case you haven't noticed, I haven't had to tell you one since yesterday, dear hexed one. I do believe I am making progress. Now, off I go to play fetch with a werewolf and an alien hunter. Ta-ta!

"Pearl's eagerness to go out onto the ice has everything to do with either her being closer to a fresh lunch or having the ability to push Orwin into the lake for laughs," I said wryly to Piper before we each took a dressing room. "Let's hope etiquette wins out in both situations."

Chapter Six

"…YOU DIDN'T HAVE to come in today."

"I told you that helping you and the animals gives me a sense of purpose," Marilyn Dorsey replied to the woman who could only be Esther. The two women were actually bundled up and walking around the corner of a barn that Piper and I initially had a bit of trouble locating since leaving the trading post. "All I would be doing at home is thinking of Ronnie and how much I miss him being there already."

Piper and I exchanged startled glances. Marilyn did not sound like a woman who might have gone off the deep end and shoved her husband into a frozen lake to drown. We had to walk a good ten minutes to the west of town to find the animal shelter, which turned out to be a two-story house on an acre of land that housed a couple of newly refurbished barns covered in metal siding to maintain the red barn look. They were presumably the outbuildings for the rescued animals. The facility was modern and clean with white crushed stone surrounding all the buildings and the small parking lot to maintain a professional appearance.

There were sounds of a number of dogs barking in a distance, with the occasional other animal sounds that made it clear domestic animals weren't the only ones who'd found a sanctuary here with Esther. There were goats, horses, cows, pigs, cats, and I'm sure other rescues that were roaming the enclosures and pens. Some were certain to be housed inside the barns, while others were enjoying the fresh air, although all of the animals had access to covered shelter, water, and food. It was easy to see that Esther ran a tight ship around here, and my heart warmed at the telltale signs that all the recues were taken care of properly.

"Excuse us," Piper called out with a wave of her knitted mitten. "Are you Esther? We were hoping to register early for the polar bear plunge tomorrow."

I maintained my focus on Marilyn, not wanting to miss any of her reactions. Had we known the shelter was located almost a mile out of town, we would have driven the Jeep. No one in the village said anything about the long hike.

"Yes, I'm Esther," the woman greeted us with a big smile. No one bothered to take off their gloves or mittens to shake hands. Someone had mentioned that the winds were supposed to pick up later this evening, but I'm pretty sure the meteorologist had been off by a good twelve hours. I lifted the hood of my coat so that a gust didn't cause my right cheek to freeze with the kiss of the biting wind. "I'm so sorry, but registration opens tomorrow morning at seven o'clock sharp. I'm sure you understand, but we can't make special exceptions for only a few."

Well, that particular rule was going to make it harder to donate to the animal shelter without us actually taking part in the main event. I would somehow figure a way out of it, but Marilyn was my main focus right now. It would certainly help to have Orwin here to read the thoughts of Esther and Marilyn, so our best bet right now was to stall until Pearl worked her magic.

I could come up with good puns too, not that anyone was around to hear me.

"I'm happy to know that you're supporting our efforts here, though," Esther said, motioning for us to head up to the house. "We rely on the funds generated by the polar bear plunge to get us through most of the year. In late summer, we even host a triathlon to bridge the gap. Where are you ladies from?"

"Pennsylvania," Piper answered, allowing me to refrain from saying Salem, Massachusetts. Every time I mentioned my hometown, it inevitably led to the old witch trial conversation. I loathed lying, although I'd gotten very good over the years at keeping secrets, or at least avoiding the whole truth. "We're actually here with two more friends, but they decided to go ice fishing early this morning. We told them to meet us here, thinking that maybe we could register early to beat the crowd tomorrow morning."

"Believe it not, the polar bear plunge usually draws about forty participants this way," Esther said with pride, quickening her pace so that she was the first to reach her porch. "This here is Marilyn. She volunteers to help me part-time, as well as some other good folks from town."

"It's nice to meet you," Piper greeted with a nod. I did the same, though my attention had been drawn somewhere to the left of us. It was almost as if I could feel the weight of someone's stare. I risked a glance in that direction, but there was just a cluster of bushes that were able to survive the harsh winters. "We think the work you do here is fantastic."

"Marilyn came over today to help organize all the paperwork for tomorrow's charity event." Esther opened her front door, motioning for us to follow. "We're sorry you walked all this way, but you mentioned that your friends are meeting you here. Come on in until they arrive. Can I get you anything? Coffee, tea, or maybe some hot cocoa?"

I was actually dying for a cup of coffee, but I didn't want to seem any ruder than we already appeared by having shown up unexpectedly. Before closing the door, I searched the thick bushes one more time in hopes of finding the person watching our every move. I didn't have any luck before we were mercifully encased with warmth behind the closed door.

"No, thank you," Piper replied, unconsciously stepping toward the heat of the blazing fire. This *was* definitely an old farmhouse that had been well taken care of in its old age. "We just had the most delicious breakfast at the diner before making a quick stop at the trading post for some thermal underwear. I have to admit it's a bit colder here than we'd expected."

Esther and Marilyn had already shed their coats, hats, and scarves. They didn't even bother to hang them up on the coatrack, but instead just threw them on top of a wooden bench that matched the rest of the living room furniture. As if the coats were a silent signal, full grown cats and kittens came out of every hiding place imaginable. Okay, maybe not that many, but there had to be at least ten or twelve felines of various lineages that all meowed at the same time.

"It's a good thing Pearl isn't here," I whispered to Piper, wondering what would happen if the scent of another cat showed up but not to the naked eye. Esther and Marilyn would certainly become wary of our visit, which meant we had to get in our questioning while we could. I spoke up so that the two women could hear me over the cats' chorus. "We're staying at the inn, and we're having such a lovely time. I'm actually a psychology professor, and the myths surrounding this place are just fascinating."

Once again, I prided myself on being truthful. I *was* a psychology professor; one taking a sabbatical in order to hunt down an immortal witch who just happened to hex me with a horrendous curse. Details. Who needed them anyway?

"Oh, you must be talking about Ominous Odessa." It was clear that Esther would have been happy to talk about the village's folklore, but her distressed gaze swept over her friend. She didn't want to hurt Marilyn's feelings. "Just so you know, Ominous Odessa is just an old wives' tale."

"I suppose you heard about the accident out on the lake," Marilyn presumed, clearing her throat before she leaned down to pet a few of the cats that had been circling her ankle. Her eyes had filled with tears before she could hide them. "That was actually my husband, Ronald Dorsey. I know the rumors circling around town, but he was a good man. He loved me, just as I loved him. Never once did he stray from our marriage. His death was simply an accident, which resulted in him being taken from this earth too soon. Some people around here have nothing better to do, though. They find it amusing to dance on their neighbor's grave."

"We're sorry to hear that, Mrs. Dorsey," Piper said softly, reaching down to pet one of the kittens who'd trotted over to us with wide, curious blue eyes. "It must be hard for you to endure these horrible rumors during such a difficult time."

Marilyn nodded her acceptance of our condolences, and I found myself truly believing that she had nothing to do with her husband's death. Her grief was real, and all I wanted now was to leave her in the caring hands of her friend. We'd already made it our mission to find her husband's killer and bring him or her to justice, but witnessing her pain at losing her soulmate was heart-wrenching.

Within the blink of an eye, almost every cat hissed in unison. Their tails became as big as round brushes, and their eyes began to dart everywhere for what I could only assume was Pearl. Her unexpected, invisible presence had gratefully switched the topic of discussion, but it had also set every feline in this house on edge.

I'll just be on my way, Pearl declared a bit haughtily. *I can see that I am not welcome here.*

"Oh, dear," Marilyn exclaimed, standing quickly and sharing an alarmed look with Esther. "What is this all about?"

The slightest rumble in the distance made itself known. Piper and I both sighed with relief when we realized that the growing and growling reverberations were from two snowmobiles. The men had not opted for Knox's Land Rover, but instead chosen to visit Henry's snowmobile rental business.

"It appears your friends have arrived," Esther replied, though there was a bit of caution in her voice as she continued to look guardedly around her living room as each cat and kitten began to relax and go about their morning as if nothing unusual had occurred. "That was very odd."

"I know it's highly unusual, but we have been known to have tremors around here. Don't get me wrong. We don't have earthquakes per se, but there was a segment on the local news regarding how they take place without any of us the wiser," Marilyn shared, scoping out the living room floor. Had I not known that the cats' reactions had everything to do with Pearl, I might have actually believed the floor was about to swallow us whole. "I've heard stories that animals are able to feel those types of natural occurrences."

"We do apologize for stopping in without notice," Piper said as I took a step back toward the door. We'd come to get a sense about Marilyn Dorsey, and I was pretty confident that she had nothing to do with her husband's fatal so-called accident out on the lake. She seemed like a really nice woman, and it wasn't fair that the guilty party should go unpunished. We certainly had our work cut out for us. "We'll be there at seven o'clock sharp tomorrow morning to register."

The engines of the snowmobiles had been turned off, and I counted in my head the amount of time it would take to walk from the gravel drive to the porch. Once I was confident that Knox and Orwin would be nearing the front door, I swung it wide open.

Both men were smiling as if they'd accomplished climbing Mt. Everest.

"That was exhilarating," Orwin exclaimed, shifting the goggles a little higher on his ski cap so that he could see better out of his black-rimmed glasses. "Henry gave us a super deal on renting two snowmobiles for the day."

Piper made the introductions after the men had walked into the house, mindful to stand on the rubber mat just inside the door. Orwin purposely took off his right glove so that he could shake hands with Esther and Marilyn, thus causing them to get in close proximity of his abilities. The unspoken plan worked like a charm, and I breathed a sigh of relief that Piper and I had come to the right conclusion about Marilyn being innocent in her husband's death. Orwin's next statement all but confirmed it.

"We heard about the death of your husband. You have our sincere condolences."

"Thank you, young man." Marilyn wasn't the type of woman who liked to have attention on her, so she quickly changed the subject. "And we appreciate your willingness to take part in the charity event for Esther's animal rescue farm."

"Yes, we do appreciate it very much," Esther reiterated, frowning when at least half of the cats had been drawn to the front window. She began to edge that way, but she'd already been close enough for Orwin to weed her out as a suspect. "What on earth is going on with my furbabies today?"

"Anything for a good cause," Orwin replied, though the spark of interest in his tone indicated that he wasn't quite done with his conversation with Esther. "We were sorry to hear that you might be selling the place."

Orwin's allegation was enough to capture Esther's interest away from the fact that the cats had figured out that Pearl might have vacated the house, but she was still close by. Esther's weathered features had turned upside down with that frown of hers.

"I am doing no such thing, and Hank should stop spreading rumors like that," Esther declared, clearly irate that others would think she would sell out for money. "There has been a gentleman around town—and I use that term lightly—who has shown interest in some of the lakeside property. He came here yesterday and was curious to see if I would sell my ten acres of land, and I told him politely that he should just pack up his carpetbags and leave town. I'm sure by now that everyone knows who he is and that he's not here for the festivities. It won't take long for Cecelia or Anne to send him packing once he's shown to be exactly who he is."

"That must be the man we saw this morning leaving the inn," I said, joining in with my two cents. We had the chance to narrow down the timetable. "Anne mentioned that he was pretty big on his privacy. I guess he's been trying to win over the trust of the town. I've seen it happen before, and these corporations love to turn small towns such as yours into commercial resort areas. It's a shame, because it's the history of villages that make them special."

Orwin's eyes widened a bit, and a spike of adrenaline

went through me that he'd finally discovered a lead in the case. It could have either come from Esther or Marilyn, but he'd heard something in their thoughts that could possibly have us solving this murder mystery before I had to immerse myself in a frigid lake and turn myself into a popsicle.

"You don't need to concern yourselves about it," Esther advised, determination taking over her previous frown. "You'll be able to come for the polar bear plunge next year and the year after that. There's not one single resident in this town who would let our history be bulldozed by some huge corporation. Hank is just a worrywart. Don't you pay any attention to his ramblings, especially when he's sitting on his seat at the tavern. He drinks too much for his own good."

"Well, we should be on our way," I said, bringing our visit to an end. It was time to have one of our meetings to share with each other what we'd all found out in the course of our mornings. "Again, we're sorry that we stopped by unannounced. We're just used to registering early in order to avoid the crowd the day of the event."

"Understandable." Esther clapped her hands together and took a step forward, prompting Knox to open the door and step out onto the porch. I hadn't realized just how much heat Esther's fireplace gave off until I was back outside in the bitter cold temperature. "I wonder what has Patsy all up in a fuss."

I now had a pretty good idea about what had been hiding in the bushes. A white miniature goat was running from snowmobile to snowmobile, hopping on the seats and then immediately jumping off...as if he were chasing something invisible.

Well, this cretin certainly isn't chasing his own shadow. It was either deal with this annoying miniature beast or face down two dozen of my own kind. An easy pick, considering those felines know all of my tricks.

Patsy must have figured out which snowmobile that Pearl had settled onto, for the goat attempted a back kick that would have done her parents proud. Etiquette went out the window when Pearl might have uttered an expletive that normally would have caused her whiskers to curl.

I'm leaving you all here to deal with this kick-happy maniac. I expect a spot of warm cream upon your arrival back at the inn. There should be hazard pay for the things we go through to solve these murder mysteries.

Chapter Seven

"RONALD DORSEY *WAS* talking to George Nektar about selling his lakeside property," Orwin revealed an hour later after we'd all returned to the inn. Both Knox and Orwin had utilized the shower to warm up and get the smell off them after their morning on the frozen lake. They were completely satisfied with themselves, given a job well done in the ice fishing department even though they'd used the catch and release method. "I picked that tidbit up from Marilyn. It was easy to detect her doubt over whether or not her husband would have actually followed through with the sale."

The best part about the first level of the inn was where the hearth was positioned, set a bit back from the main lobby. We were able to carry on a private conversation while sitting on the numerous couches and chairs, all the while keeping an eye on the front entrance. Pearl had done a quick sweep of the town after having a small portion of catnip to calm herself after her encounter with Patsy. She discovered that Mr. Nektar was currently in talks with Charles Jounce. Apparently, the elderly man owned the largest lakefront property near the existing wharf.

These residents have nothing to fear, dear hexed one. Mr. Jounce might be in his eighties, but he's sharp as a tack. If I hadn't known any better, I would have sworn he'd even caught on to my presence. He's one of those individuals who are very attuned with his surroundings.

"We stopped into the trading post after breakfast," Piper shared, sipping the cup of hot tea she'd made in our room. Pearl was near the fireplace in her invisible state, no doubt allowing the calming effects of her catnip to do its job. "Hank was upset that Henry would even consider selling his building, though he claimed that he just told Mr. Nektar that he'd think over his offer in order to get him to leave the shop."

I will have you know that I ingested only a pinch of the minty herb. I'm well within my limitations, dear hexed one.

"And we also ran into Wallace, who couldn't even bring himself to go out onto the ice this morning." I settled back into the warmth of the leather, wondering how much it would cost to replace the chairs in the RV with something as comfortable as these cushions. Standard RV furniture wasn't the best when it came to comfort, but I could definitely upgrade our custom rig. "His grief seemed palpable."

I do believe that the lumberjack lookalike is just a big teddy bear at heart, unlike that wicked kicking cretin at Ms. Esther's place.

"What was more interesting was the fact that we met Marilyn's aunt," Piper chimed back in, casting her gaze toward where Anne was entering the office on the opposite side of the room. "She clearly believes that Mr. Dorsey was having an affair with Debra Lily. Ms. Rusco didn't appear sad in the least that he was dead."

"You'll have to figure out a way to get close to Ms. Rusco later this evening. She mentioned taking Marilyn to the diner for fish tacos, so maybe we can head back there around five or six o'clock tonight." I did not want to believe that Marilyn's aunt had the ability to murder someone, but we had pretty much witnessed some crazy things since the beginning our little chase for justice. "After this morning's explorations, I'm not sure which motive I'm leaning toward."

"I think we need to rule out George Nektar first." Knox was sitting across from me. His five o'clock shadow only seemed to highlight the fact that his cheeks were a bit wind chapped, though the redness was fading. His ability to heal was quite amazing. "Let's hope he makes his way back to the inn. Orwin can do his thing, then we can move on to other suspects."

"...won't do that," Cecelia exclaimed in irritation, her voice carrying across the room. "Yes, we agreed that we don't want that type of guest, but I'm sure he'll leave soon enough when no one takes him up on his company's dirty money. Leave well enough alone, Anne."

"But Mom, he's trying to systematically destroy our

town," Anne replied, her frustration showing even more than her mother's as they came storming out of the office. "How can we let someone like that stay here with us?"

Cecelia must have noticed us near the hearth. She didn't reply to her daughter, but instead began to put on her jacket and scarf, all but abandoning their conversation. It didn't take her long to storm out the front entrance, apparently needing a bit of a breather from her daughter. Anne's huff of frustration could easily be heard, and it didn't take her long to go back into the office and slam the door shut a bit too loud. We were too far away for Orwin to have picked up on their thoughts.

"So, the game plan is to wait for Mr. Nektar to come back to the inn so that Orwin can rule him out as a suspect and then kill some time until we can walk over to the diner." Knox grimaced at his own choice of words. "We were able to talk to a lot of ice fishermen today, plus Hank and Henry. Orwin was also able to eliminate all of them from the suspect pool."

Although Knox and Orwin had fun in their extracurricular activities, they had gotten a lot of work done on the case. Still, I had to wonder if I wouldn't find myself encased in a block of ice come morning.

You'll just have to keep reminding yourself that the polar bear plunge is for a good cause, dear hexed one. On the bright side, you can enjoy a spot of warm cream with me afterward. They do have some premium cream from the local dairy farms.

"Orwin said that Marilyn couldn't stop thinking about her husband's meetings with Mr. Nektar. We've already seen how the other residents are reacting to the offers he's making for lakefront property and the various buildings around town, so I'm thinking that has to be the motive." Piper took another sip of her tea. "A wife usually knows when her husband is unfaithful. If Marilyn was confident in her husband's fidelity, then his willingness to sell out had to be the only motive for his murder."

All of us seemed to agree with Piper's theory, although we couldn't completely rule out Ms. Rusco's role if she truly believed she was protecting her niece.

"Even with those we've eliminated today in consideration of that motive, that still leaves the majority of the townsfolk as suspects," Orwin said, clearly itching to walk around town in hopes of catching a floating thought or two regarding what we knew to be Mr. Dorsey's murder. "Let's give Mr. Nektar ten more minutes to come back to the inn. If Pearl is right about Mr. Jounce's views on the subject of selling his property, the meeting shouldn't last long."

As if right on cue, the front entrance swung open to reveal George Nektar. He didn't even bother to look in our direction, which meant he was heading straight to his room, probably to generate an email to update his corporate office.

I've got this, my dear colleagues.

I wasn't sure what Pearl had in mind to prevent Mr. Nektar from going upstairs, but the delay did give me a chance to clarify something with Orwin.

"Orwin, did Marilyn give you any indication that she was thinking of following through with her husband's wishes to sell their lakefront property?"

"No, not at all. It was the complete opposite." Orwin stopped talking when Mr. Nektar tripped on what appeared to be midair and almost went headfirst into the area rug. Pearl had certainly done an excellent job of delaying him. "Mrs. Dorsey actually called Mr. Nektar and told him that she was not interested in selling, because all she had left of her husband was their home."

Job well done, if I do say so myself. I'll be curled up near the warm fire should you need my services for anything else, dear colleagues.

It hit me as we all got to our feet to help Mr. Nektar off the floor that he'd been conducting business underneath the radar with Mr. Dorsey. It wasn't until the man's death that he'd stopped skulking around, thereby giving up his true identity. Did that mean someone had actually bitten on the bait that Mr. Nektar had thrown to the residents?

"There's only one way to find out," Orwin murmured in reply to my thought. By this time, we were right behind Piper as she knelt next to Mr. Nektar. "Showtime."

"Are you alright, sir?" Piper asked, having set her tea

down on the coffee table before hurrying to Mr. Nektar's aid. "You must have tripped over the rug. You're lucky you didn't hit your head on the step!"

"I'm fine, I'm fine," Mr. Nektar reassured us, wincing when he leaned down to put his hand on his knee. "Although I might have banged up my knee a bit."

Piper was keeping her hand on Mr. Nektar's arm a little longer than usual, alerting us to the fact that there wouldn't be a scratch on the man by the time he left our presence. You see, whereas my ability was honed to telekinesis and Orwin's to telepathy, our youngest witch had the ability to heal. Granted, she was still in the learning stages, but she was getting better with each patient.

I glanced toward the office, hoping that Anne wouldn't come out to see what all the fuss was about anytime soon. We needed a minute alone with Mr. Nektar.

"Should we get Anne or Cecelia?" I asked, making an attempt to advance toward the office, already knowing that Mr. Nektar wouldn't want the additional attention. "If you need to go to the—"

"No, no!" Mr. Nektar replied adamantly, his insistence at making sure that the Dahls weren't aware of this incident confirming my suspicion. He knew his time in this town was coming to an end, and he was afraid that the Dahls would tell him that today was that day. "I'm fine."

Mr. Nektar peered around Knox and Orwin to see if it truly was the rug that had caused his stumble. Knox shifted to the right slightly so that the man's vision was blocked, giving Orwin time pick up any guilt or innocence that was forefront in Mr. Nektar's mind.

"Are you here for the ice fishing competition?" Piper asked, finally releasing her hold on Mr. Nektar's arm. "We're here for the polar bear plunge. Did you know that all the proceeds go to the animal shelter? You should really join in for such a great cause."

"Oh, I don't think that kind of activity is for me." Mr. Nektar lifted a hand to his black hair, which was practically cement after having a few flurries land on whatever product he'd lathered into the strands this morning. "I have a phone call to make, so if you'll excuse me. I do appreciate your help, though."

Piper and I stepped aside so that Mr. Nektar could continue to his room. We all observed him as he took the steps one by one, eventually disappearing down the hallway. He never once looked back toward us, his sole focus on that phone call he needed to make.

"Mr. Nektar didn't murder Ronald Dorsey." Orwin had gotten right to the point, pushing up his black-rimmed glasses as we made our way back to our seats. Piper grabbed her tea before settling onto the couch, and now I was wishing that I'd made myself a cup of coffee. There was a small table behind us that served as a refreshment bar, and I was tempted to use the Keurig machine. First, I wanted to hear what Orwin had to say. "You can take him off the suspect list, Piper. He—"

Orwin stopped midsentence while attempting to control his allergies. He was unsuccessful and sneezed four times before taking the tissue that Knox had grabbed from the wooden box on the coffee table. We all shared knowing looks.

"You're right behind my head, aren't you, Pearl?" Orwin muttered, motioning for Knox to change seats with him. Orwin had taken the overstuffed chair closest to the fire, which was probably why Pearl had decided that would be the coziest place to curl up on for her afternoon snooze. "Of all the places you could have taken a nap?"

I'm not the one who arranged the furniture in the room, alien hunter. Now continue with your findings so that I may retire upstairs for the remainder of my nap. That blanket is just divine! We may just have to take it with us, which means one of you will need to convince Ms. Dahl to sell it to us for a reasonable price.

"I know this is a foolish question, but is he really trying to buy his company's way into this town?" Piper asked, sadness lacing her tone as she held her tea with one hand while working her phone with the other. She was rearranging the suspect list on her Murder 101 app, and I was curious as to see who was still front and center. "This village has something really special. It would be a shame to see it all go corporate."

"Mr. Nektar did locate the weak link in the group,

which just so happened to be Mr. Dorsey." Orwin finished blowing his nose and tossing the used tissue into a small wastebasket off to the side. "Let's just say he isn't happy that Marilyn won't budge on selling after her husband's previous verbal commitment."

"Why was Mr. Nektar in a rush to make that call just now?" I asked, though Orwin's reply was delayed when our attention focused on Anne coming out of the office. She was talking in hushed tones on her cell phone, and she seemed quite upset as she walked past the front desk and down to their private rooms that we knew were on the first floor. "I wonder what that was about."

We waited a moment, hoping to see Anne reappear, but the inn had become rather quiet in the last few seconds. The only noise that was echoing around the first floor were the shifting logs in the fireplace that were producing rising embers from the flames.

"To answer your previous question, Mr. Nektar wanted to reach out to his boss for some tax information regarding the tavern." Orwin's concerned frown told us the seriousness of the situation. "Apparently, Mr. Jounce mentioned that Trout was having financial troubles. Mr. Nektar is hoping to capitalize on that information."

Hank was right earlier this morning when he said this town was made up of dominos. All it took was for one key owner to fall, and there would be a chain reaction faster than Pearl's ability to disappear into thin air.

I wouldn't say that, dear hexed one, but I did decide to delay my much-needed slumber in order to take a stroll around the inn. There is a valid reason that Miss Dahl is upset, and it has to do with one Mr. Wallace Turnhill.

"Wallace? As in Mr. Dorsey's best friend?" Piper leaned forward, setting her cell phone in her lap. "What happened?"

It appears as if our resident lumberjack had an accident of his own. He's on his way to the hospital now after his snowmobile lost control near the wharf, and he's claiming that his throttle was suddenly stuck wide open. Coincidence? I think not, dear colleagues.

Chapter Eight

"WHAT IF WE'RE looking about this case all wrong? What if it has nothing to do with Mr. Nektar?" Piper asked quietly from behind her scarf. We'd all gotten fortified with our outer gear, using the two snowmobiles to get us to the wharf as quickly as possible. "Mr. Dorsey and Mr. Turnhill were best friends. What if this has something to do with them specifically?"

"We could be focusing too much on the most convenient motive," Knox pointed out, "but why else would those two be specifically targeted? Marilyn doesn't believe her husband cheated on her, so that pretty much resolved what we initially believed was the only other reason for Dorsey's murder."

You might want to inform Mr. Emeric that we have yet to rule out Ms. Rusco. That woman strikes me as the type to go to extreme lengths to protect her family. I daresay she reminds me a little of you, dear hexed one.

Knox only had his jacket on, though the scarf that Piper had knitted him hung loose around his neck. His body temperature ran high, given that he was affected with lycanthropy. The cold didn't bother him in the slightest, while the three of us were practically shivering as the gusts of winds pierced through even our new thermal underwear.

The delicious scents coming from that direction are quite intoxicating, are they not? In case you hadn't noticed, dear hexed one, we have skipped lunch.

An older gentleman in uniform, who could only be Sheriff Torkin, was standing next to a man who knew exactly how to dress for this brutal weather. He didn't seem to be the least bit affected by the bitter cold winds either, as he leaned over what was left of Wallace's burned-out snowmobile.

"That's Albert," Orwin replied, advancing close enough to us that he'd heard my curiosity on what was taking place near the dock. "He's the town's mechanic. I was able to walk by them under the ruse of speaking with Henry regarding our snowmobile rentals. I've booked them through tomorrow, by the way."

I appreciate that, alien hunter. These oversized machines give me a place to sit, thereby allowing my paws a brief respite from the cold.

"What did Albert and the sheriff have on their minds?" I asked, wishing that I'd bought those hand warmers I'd seen next to the cash register at the trading post. I made a mental note to stop there on our way back to the inn. "Do they believe someone tampered with Wallace's snowmobile?"

"Well, all that is on the sheriff's mind is how this

accident could affect Henry's business for the tourist season." Orwin's nose was quite red, and this time it had nothing to do with Pearl and her dander. "He hasn't made any correlation at all between Dorsey's murder and Wallace's accident."

"Maybe there isn't one," Piper commented, stepping around Orwin so that he was the one to take the brunt of the wind. "Wallace could have simply had an accident."

"I highly doubt that." Orwin adjusted his black ski cap and stared at the mechanic through his black-rimmed glasses. "Albert seemed confident that someone fiddled with the return spring on Wallace's throttle."

Cutting a person's throttle return takes someone without a speck of morals. Perhaps we should be more cautious from this point on. We wouldn't want the murderer to know that we believe Mr. Dorsey's death wasn't an accident, either.

I couldn't figure out why two best friends would be targeted, leaving their murder and attempted murder to look like accidents. Had they been doing something illegal? We'd just assumed the secretive meetings that Ronald Dorsey had been having were with Mr. Nektar instead of Debra Lily. What if we were wrong on both counts?

I could go pay Mr. Turnhill a visit at the hospital to monitor his visitors.

One of our rules as a traveling group of hunters was that no one ever went anywhere alone. Pearl following Mr. Nektar the other day had been allowed only because she'd done so from afar with the unspoken promise of remaining invisible and at a distance at all times. I wasn't too keen on allowing her to go inside a hospital where she could become trapped.

Mr. Turnhill is not of the supernatural, dear hexed one. Now that isn't to say there isn't a spirit or two roaming the halls who might take exception to my presence, but I assure you that I can be discreet.

"Well, we're not going to solve this murder mystery by standing around here." Knox motioned toward the snowmobiles. "Let's head back to town. We can stop at the pub for a bit to see if Orwin can pick up any more leads on Trout's financial problems."

As we all began to crowd around the two vehicles, I instructed Pearl to stay with us. If Wallace hadn't been hurt too badly, chances were that he'd be back in town within the hour. The faintest sound of music could be heard drifting on the fringes of the wind, and I tilted my head to see if I recognized the song. Within seconds, the light resonance had dissipated with one of the strong gusts.

"Lou?" Knox called my name, his dark eyes studying my face as if to make sure that I was okay. "Are you hopping on the back or are you hiking it back to town?"

Hiking it back to town was debatable, considering it would only take five minutes to reach the tavern by foot. We'd driven the snowmobiles for two reasons—we'd rented them, and they were incredibly fun.

Your idea of fun should be analyzed a bit more, dear hexed one. I opt not to travel on the same vehicle that a resident of this village just used to crash into the wharf, thank you very much. I shall meet you all at the pub.

"I was just trying to see where the music was coming from." I took the goggles that Knox handed me and slipped them over my ski cap. He gave me another perplexed look, but he might not have heard the song while he was mounting the snowmobile, though his hearing was vastly superior to mine. Orwin had already started his engine with Piper right behind him, and they didn't waste time heading back to town. "It's no big deal. It sounded familiar, and I was just trying to remember where I'd heard it before. Let's go."

It didn't take us long to reach the pub, though it was rather sparse given the time of day. Knox turned off the engine, but we didn't bother getting off the snowmobile. Orwin and Piper had already walked inside and determined that it would be futile for us to waste our time. Not even Trout was bartending, though he was expected to show up around four o'clock. In the meantime, that left us with few options.

You spoke to soon, dear hexed one.

"What's the next best thing to a diner to get all the local gossip?" Piper asked, posing a setting that none of us wanted to find ourselves in. Her bright smile only confirmed our suspicions. "Oh, you guys. Come on. Look at all the things I've made you already, and I've only just scratched the surface!"

I'm not so sure why Pearl sounded so upbeat. She

was the one who complained about the winter booties that Piper had knitted her for Christmas, though not in Piper's presence. Sure, a joke or two was made about Piper's obsession with knitting, but Pearl was too much of an etiquette queen to be rude. In Pearl's defense, I wouldn't want to walk around in manmade boots if I was a cat, either.

"I overheard one of women at the diner talk about the knitting store on the opposite end of town. Get this—it's also a tea shop!" Piper exclaimed, pulling her goggles over her blue eyes for the added protection. She motioned for Orwin to hop back on the snowmobile. "We'll meet you there."

For once, I'm all for paying a visit to a local knitting shop. For this particular one to incorporate a tea shop into their business, they deserve a bit of recognition. It's teatime, dear hexed one!

We could only watch in dismay from our own seats as the two took off down the street. I had no doubt that Pearl was close behind, if not already at the knitting shop's entrance. Piper wasn't wrong about the knitting circles and tea drinkers in towns such as this one. We'd witnessed firsthand in our last case how much those ladies knew about the latest chinwag that was being turned out by the gossip mill.

"Do we really need—"

"Shhh." I even held up my hand to stop Knox from saying another word, having once again caught the faintest sounds of that familiar song I'd heard down by the wharf. "You don't hear that music?"

Knox looked over his shoulder at me, his own pair of goggles still positioned high up on his forehead. He shook his head after attempting to listen for a minute. I strained to catch the light tune now being drowned out by a passing car.

"Never mind," I said, dismissing the issue at hand. "It stopped. Hey, do you mind if we walk to the trading post? They had those hand warmers that we can stick in our gloves."

"Sure," Knox agreed, even though he wouldn't need the creative gizmos. He waited until I swung my leg over the back so that I was standing next to him. "It will also give us a chance to see why Mr. Nektar is heading in that direction, as well."

I peered over Knox's shoulder, shocked to find that I'd completely missed Mr. Nektar walking by as he came from the direction of the inn. He seemed rather determined, which meant a small detour for us. I motioned for Knox to hurry as I quickly texted Piper our change in plans. Those two could pay a visit to the knitting shop in search of some interesting gossip. Knox and I would follow Mr. Nektar in hopes of a new discovery.

When Mr. Nektar turned left at the intersection, Knox and I glanced at each other in curiosity. We had yet to venture down the side roads of the village, so we had no idea what we would be heading into if we blindly followed behind our target.

"We know for a fact that George Nektar didn't murder Ronald Dorsey, so I'm not sure it's worth following him." Knox gave his opinion, and I happened to agree. With that said, I loathed seeing the residents in this town being taken advantage of by some corporate hack who wasn't beneath blackmail to earn a dollar. "We're following him anyway, aren't we?"

"Orwin believes Trout is a great guy after spending time at the pub last night," I said with a shrug. "How can we ignore the fact that he's about to be blackmailed out of his own bar?"

By this time, we'd turned the corner to find that Mr. Nektar was receiving some sort of envelope from a very surprising individual—Anne Dahl. We hastily retreated back around the corner so that we wouldn't be spotted, though neither one of us quite believed what we'd just witnessed, as we were completely aware of how Anne felt about the man.

"We should have kept Pearl with us," Knox whispered, standing in front of me to make it appear that we were having a conversation. My cheeks and nose had to be quite red by now from the crosswind, because they'd pretty much gone numb. "Is there a way to call her back?"

Knox might be a werewolf, but it had been due to a hex. What he knew about the supernatural was what he'd learned from us, but to really know the ins and outs of magic…well, that type of knowledge would take years.

"Trust me," I whispered back, motioning for Knox to take another peek around the side of the building. "Pearl is enjoying her spot of warm cream, and she isn't going anywhere until she laps up every last drop. We're on our own, but I might have an idea. Tell me when George Nektar is walking back this way. Oh, and be ready to look inside that envelope."

I readied myself for what had to be done, knowing that it was going to smart as bad as stubbing my toe on the end of the bed this morning. Truthfully, I expected to be waiting for a while, but Knox gave me the nod that it was showtime. I motioned for him to lower his head so that I could use the reflection off his goggles to gauge the distance between us and Mr. Nektar. When the time was right, I quickly stepped out from my hiding place and ran smack dab into the man, flicking my wrist so that he lost his grip on the envelope.

"Oh!" I exclaimed as both of us lost our balance. We went tumbling to the ground in a pile of arms and legs, giving Knox the ability to chase after the envelope that had been conveniently carried away on a gust of wind. I took it upon myself to keep Mr. Nektar busy while Knox got a good look at the contents. "I'm so sorry. I turned the corner and slipped on an ice spot. Are you okay? Goodness gracious, twice in one day."

Mr. Nektar was doing his best to stand, though I was

purposefully making that a bit difficult for him. Every time he went to stand, I feigned slipping on the sidewalk.

"I'm fine," Mr. Nektar said in frustration, practically gritting his teeth together when I once again landed him right back down on his buttocks. "Are you okay? If you'd stop moving, I can stand and then help you up."

Knox had to go a ways down the sidewalk to snatch up the envelope, so I made sure that he was walking back in our direction before I did as Mr. Nektar suggested. He was out of breath by the time he stood up, though he did reach down to assist me. I guess he couldn't be all that bad, but I still didn't like the fact that he was taking advantage of the residents.

Was that what Anne Dahl had been doing? Attempting to get rid of him with a little blackmail herself? I wouldn't find out until Knox returned the envelope to Mr. Nektar and sent the man on his way.

"Here you go," Knox replied, handing over the object in question. "The wind carried it down the sidewalk, but I was able to retrieve it before it was lost."

"I appreciate that," Mr. Nektar said, his frown practically a permanent part of his face since I'd first seen him this morning. "Clearly, today isn't my day. Are you sure you are okay, miss?"

"Yes," I responded, swiping my gloves against each other to get the grit off them. "With this jacket, I'm padded all over the place. Didn't even feel a thing."

"Good, good." Mr. Nektar gave me the once over, as

if to reassure himself that no damage had been done in our collision. "Well, I best be off. I have some business to attend to."

Knox and I both remained silent until Mr. Nektar turned the corner.

"Well?" I asked, unable to wait a second longer to find out what was in that envelope. "What did Anne Dahl give Mr. Nektar?"

"First, you're not going to believe it," Knox said rather cagily, following up his statement with a similar one. "And second, you're going to hate it."

"Spill," I ordered, tilting my head slightly to the right when I thought I'd caught the faintest sound of that familiar song again. I must have it stuck in my head, because all I could hear now was the sound of my own breathing. "What was in that envelope?"

I can't leave you two alone for five minutes, can I? I will say that the brand of cream those ladies enjoy at the knitting shop was quite the treat. They spare no expense for their customers. Now that I'm fully satiated, I too would like to hear what was in the mystifying envelope.

"One thousand dollars in cash."

"What?" I couldn't have heard correctly, because a thousand dollars was nothing to sneeze at. How would Anne Dahl get her hands on that kind of money, anyway? A horrible thought crossed my mind, but I immediately retracted it. "Did you say a thousand dollars in cash?"

"I didn't stutter," Knox said, having no idea that

Pearl had joined the conversation. He was too busy stepping forward to see where Mr. Nektar had run off to with all that cash. "The question is why did Anne give him that much money? Was it a payoff of some sort?"

You might as well say what we're all thinking, dear hexed one. It's a bit extreme, but all evidence points toward Miss Dahl hiring Mr. Nektar to do away with Ronald Dorsey and Wallace Turnhill. I do believe this murder mystery has taken quite an interesting turn.

Chapter Nine

"THAT MAKES NO sense," Orwin replied in disbelief after hearing what Knox and I had to say. We'd met up back at the inn, taking up residence in the sitting area next to the massive hearth. "Why on earth would Anne give that man a thousand dollars? And don't you dare say it was to hire out a contract on two men she's known her whole life. I most definitely would have picked something up regarding an act that horrible when I was standing right in front of her last night."

Not to point out the obvious, alien hunter, but you were rather caught up in the enlightening conversation you were having outside with those two strangers about the possibility of there being an unidentified flying object at the bottom of the lake. Mistakes do happen.

I hadn't thought about it in those terms, but Pearl did have a point. There about a lot going on last night when we entered the inn.

"No, Pearl does not have a point," Orwin denied, pushing up his black-rimmed glasses and shooting me a disbelieving glare through the lenses. "Anne Dahl is obsessed with Ominous Odessa. That's who she truly believes got her slimy fingers on Dorsey right before he took a dive into that freezing water. There wasn't one stray thought that indicated she would hire someone to murder two men. I'm pretty sure something like that would have been forefront in her thoughts while we were asking about his demise."

"The quickest way to know is to wait right here until Anne makes an appearance," Piper said, doing her best to mediate. Orwin and Pearl had quite the complicated love/hate relationship. Honestly, it all depended on the day. "I caught a glimpse of Cecelia in the office talking on the phone. It's almost check-in time, and I'm sure that a guest is bound to arrive for one of the festivities tomorrow. Anne should be here soon."

I wasn't about to waste the opportunity to grab some coffee, so I quickly made my way to the small refreshment table. I still hadn't had time to stop at the trading post for those hand warmers, but it was at the top of my to-do list. Right now, the warm fire and a hot cup of coffee would warm up my bones.

I had just set the carafe back on the burner when the sound of a thud echoed throughout the lower level. A glance over my shoulder revealed someone coming down the staircase, and it was none other than George Nektar...with suitcase in hand.

The pieces of the man's secretive meeting began to fall into place, but had Anne simply paid him to leave town or had she paid him for services rendered and his job here was now done?

"Mr. Nektar?" Cecelia had ended her phone call and now stood at the threshold of her office. A frown marred her face, and she seemed to have no idea why one of her guests was leaving earlier than his check-out date. "Is there a problem?"

"No, no, not at all," George replied, finally making it down the stairs as he juggled with his suitcase, briefcase, and his winter jacket. "I'm just needed back home. I understand if you need to charge me for the rest of my stay."

"Emergencies are understandable," Cecelia reassured him, stepping behind the desk so that she could close his account. "We have your credit card on file, so you're all set. I hope you have a safe trip back."

George glanced our way, but he didn't even bother to raise a hand in goodbye. The exchange had happened so quick that Orwin had only made it halfway across the so-called lobby. He hastily managed to get in front of George under the guise of being a gentleman to hold open the door. George took his time putting on his winter coat, thus giving time for Orwin to remain within the six feet that was required of his gift to read the man's thoughts.

I slowly made my way back to the couch, all the while keeping my gaze on Orwin. He was nodding to something that George had said on his way out, and eventually the door closed behind his departure. The cold draft eventually reached us, and I could have sworn I'd heard the music from earlier coming with it, playing as if it had never stopped.

"Anne paid him to leave town," Orwin announced, beaming that he'd been right about his previous reading of the young woman. He pushed his black-rimmed glasses up the bridge of his nose as he settled back into his chair, flashing us a smile of contentment. "One for the alien hunter, zero for the Egyptian cotton ball."

Is that how we're playing the game, Mr. Cornelia? Duly noted.

Orwin's smile slipped just a bit, probably recalling the time his cereal bowl had mysteriously spilled its contents onto his keyboard. The two always seemed to know how to up the ante.

"I still think he's the key to Mr. Dorsey's murder," I murmured behind my cup of coffee, switching my focus to Cecelia. She was still behind the desk. "Orwin, why don't you go talk to Cecelia? Maybe she suspects something about Anne paying Mr. Nektar to leave town. I don't like the fact that he spent weeks here doing everything possible to get these residents to cave on selling their property, only to be bribed with a mere one thousand dollars to leave town. That makes no sense."

"On it." Orwin stood, but he didn't get farther than the edge of the large area rug. Anne came barreling through the front door, humming a song as if she was the happiest woman in Pikeville. She flashed a smile Orwin's way. "Isn't today just beautiful? I heard you went ice fishing. Did you catch anything?"

Orwin began speaking with Anne about his trip out on the ice, even bringing up the tale about the UFO plunging to the depth of the lake many, many years ago. We all sighed in resignation, figuring we'd be sitting here for a while. Not only was Orwin being given the ability to confirm his suspicions about Anne's innocence, but UFO conspiracies were his favorite topic.

I made the mistake of telling our resident conspiracy theorist the other day that I met JFK once. I'm relatively sure that he is composing a list of questions for me. It's why I've been doing my best to antagonize him recently, dear hexed one. It wouldn't behoove me to go around spilling state secrets, now would it?

Piper giggled before relaying to Knox what Pearl's agenda had been lately with riling Orwin up about his abilities. I was still trying to figure out how to solve this murder mystery by tonight. I really, really wasn't looking forward to jumping into a vast body of freezing water.

"Should we head over to the diner?" Knox asked, not having to glance at a watch to tell the time. Werewolves had the uncanny ability to know exactly what time of day it was at any given moment. I, on the other hand, had to look at the antique grandfather clock in the corner. Sure enough, it was dinnertime. "Once we rule out Ms. Rusco as a suspect, we can put our heads together to plan our next steps."

We waited patiently for Orwin to finish up his conversation with Anne, who was currently being summoned into the office by her mother. We could all sense the anger coming off the woman in waves. It didn't take a genius to guess that Cecelia had somehow come to the conclusion that Anne was the one responsible for Mr. Nektar's departure.

"Anne paid Mr. Nektar one thousand dollars for the sole purpose that he leave this town. She believes that she was protecting her mother and the village," Orwin shared as we joined him in the middle of the lobby. "She's very pleased that her plan worked out."

"We noticed," I replied wryly, trying to drink as much of my coffee as I could before we walked over to the diner. I tossed the disposable cup into the small wastebasket near the door, taking time to zip up my coat. "Would you guys go grab a booth? I want to stop into the trading post to pick up those hand warmers."

I will escort you, dear hexed one.

We all took time to put on our gloves and hats, sans Knox. He just zipped up his leather jacket that he'd exchanged for the thicker coat he'd worn ice fishing this morning. There was no need to take the snowmobile when the diner was simply across the street and down one block.

The three of them immediately crossed the street while I continued down the sidewalk toward the trading post with the promise of picking up a couple of hand warmers for Piper. Don't think it hadn't crossed my mind to buy the entire box and line them up against my skin before jumping into the water tomorrow morning if we didn't happen to solve this murder mystery.

I don't claim to be a scientist, Miss Lilura, but I'm relatively sure that the ingredients in those pouches don't mix well with freezing water.

"You're not helping," I muttered behind my scarf, once again picking up the faintest sounds of music as the song traveled through the air. "Do you recognize that song?"

Song?

"Yes, do you recognize the song that's been playing on and off all day?" I reiterated, quickening my steps so that I could reach the trading post a bit faster. The meteorologist was right about the wind picking up. "They better not have sold out of those hand warmers."

I don't hear anything, dear hexed one, except the loud engine on that truck about to make a left turn at the intersection.

I'd finally reached the entrance to the trading post. I didn't hesitate to quickly enter the store, agreeing that the earsplitting rumble of the engine drowned out all other sounds. If I was lucky, the song might still be playing when we made our way over to the diner.

"Hi, Mr. Sampson," I greeted, making my way directly to the counter where I'd seen the box of hand warmers. What I had not expected was to see Sheriff Torkin leaning against the counter with a cup of steaming hot coffee in his hand. It was in a ceramic mug, so Mr. Sampson must have poured him a fresh cup. "Oh. Sorry. I didn't mean to interrupt."

Now is your chance to find out what the good ol' sheriff discovered about Mr. Turnhill's snowmobile accident, dear hexed one. Make good use of this encounter.

"No interruption at all," Mr. Sampson replied with a smile. "What can I do for you? I hope those thermal underwear worked out well for you."

"I still have them on," I quipped, letting him know that my previous purchase had been worth every penny. "I actually stopped in on my way to the diner to pick up some of those hand warmers. Anne Dahl mentioned that there was free ice skating tonight for anyone who was interested in stopping by the rink."

Here we go again, dear hexed one. I can already tell what the sheriff is about to ask you by the way he's looking you over. I really do need to find out if there is some type of contest in this town. I do so love me a bit of healthy competition.

"Let me guess," Sheriff Torkin said, narrowing his eyes to the point his black bushy eyebrows practically touched together. "You're here for the ice sculpting competition."

"Wrong." Mr. Sampson was quick to deny the sheriff's conjecture, and I had a gut feeling that Pearl might be right about the inside contest. It must be done on an honor system though, because not everyone had a witness to their predictions. "She and her friends are here for the polar bear plunge."

"Well, I have to tell you," Sheriff Torkin replied after accepting his defeat. "Those hand warmers won't come close to doing their job after you jump into that freezing water. No, siree. You'll be cold for days after that crazy stunt. I told Esther I'd just go ahead and donate to her animal shelter, but you couldn't pay me to jump into that lake. No way, no how."

Oh, my heavens! Is that what I think it is? Miss Lilura, today couldn't get any better. First, I had one of the most amazing spots of warm cream that I've enjoyed in years…and now this!

The sheriff didn't seem so bad now that I knew where he stood on insane endeavors, such as purposefully immersing oneself in freezing water. I could think of a million other things to do in order to raise money for charity.

"Didn't I see you at the wharf today?" Sheriff Torkin asked, still focusing his attention on me. I was trying not to react to whatever it was that had caught Pearl's attention. "I remember you now."

"Yes, my friends and I rented two snowmobiles from Henry," I replied, relief washing over me when I saw that the box on the counter still had some handwarmers left. Mr. Sampson was already picking two off the small pile. "We heard about the accident, though. I hope whoever was driving the snowmobile that crashed into part of the wharf is okay."

You'll need to come look at this, dear hexed one. I'm

near the camping gear.

"Wallace is fine," Sheriff Torkin responded good-naturedly, not seemingly concerned at all that the man's throttle had been messed with. "As a matter of fact, he's already home and resting. He just got a few cuts and bruises. The doctor ruled out any broken bones, so he was quite fortunate. The accident could have been much worse."

The bell above the entrance rang, letting Mr. Sampson know that he'd gotten a new customer. It was a couple who must have been locals, because they called out a hello to both the sheriff and Mr. Sampson. They walked deeper into the shop for whatever items they'd come to purchase.

"I heard Albert thought the return spring on the throttle cable had been cut through with a pair of wire cutters," Mr. Sampson interjected, raising an eyebrow when I indicated that I wanted to buy the entire box. There couldn't have been more than ten left. I had no doubt that Piper and I would use that many throughout the evening, especially if we were going to be galivanting around town looking for more leads. "Don't know who'd want to go and do a thing like that, but Albert is rarely wrong about his gadgets."

Oh, dear. No, no, no. Miss Lilura, I am not responsible for what happens if you don't come over to the camping section right this minute.

It was very unlike Pearl to focus on anything other

than the investigation, but this conversation was just getting to the good stuff. I couldn't walk away now.

"Wallace claims that his throttle was stuck wide open, and that's why Albert suggested that maybe the return spring had been cut." Sheriff Torkin took a tentative drink of his coffee, testing the temperature so that the hot beverage didn't burn the roof of his mouth. "In the end, Albert couldn't find a thing wrong with the engine. Honestly, everyone's on edge after that tragic accident on the lake last week. I'm sure you heard all about it, ma'am. We lost one of our own in a senseless mishap, a man who just happened to be Wallace's best friend."

Miss Lilura, I rarely use my abilities to frighten people, but I'm afraid I'll have little choice if this woman so much as touches the last green blanket.

Now Pearl's behavior all made sense. She'd fallen in love with the cream blanket at the inn, and it wasn't much of a surprise to find out that Cecelia or Anne had purchased some of their décor from a local shop. I had no doubt that Pearl would do whatever was necessary to get her paws on such a soft, cozy blanket to take back to the RV.

"I also wanted to pick up something else," I said, holding up my hand to pause the conversation now that I'd discovered that Wallace's accident was nothing more than that. "Give me one second."

To say that I reached the green blanket milliseconds

before the woman who had just walked in with her husband was an understatement. I shrugged my apology, not that sorry due to the abundance of other colors. The green fabric actually did match Pearl's eyes, so I understood her desire to have har favorite hue if we were going to spend...

Yes, I am well aware of the cost, but you do realize that we are supporting the local mom and pop shops, correct? Look at it as if we're just doing our part, Miss Lilura.

I managed to bite my tongue from arguing that point, because I'm pretty sure we were already doing our part by solving murder mysteries while hunting down the Lich Queen, who just so happened to have lost her sanity decades ago, if not a century.

Semantics, dear hexed one. Semantics.

"Is that all for you?" Mr. Sampson asked, ringing up the rest of the hand warmers, as well as the blanket. He put everything into a bag while I swiped my credit card, ignoring the total. That didn't stop Mr. Sampson from announcing it in front of the sheriff. "That'll be sixty-four dollars and twenty-eight cents on your American Express."

I'm well aware of how you have trouble looking for the silver lining, but in this case think of all the points you'll rack up on this month's credit card statement.

Unlike Orwin, I knew where my limitations stood in terms of going head to head with a familiar. It was rather simple, really. Familiars *always* won. It was better to forge an alliance than to make an enemy.

I've always liked the way you think, Miss Lilura.

I took the bag that Mr. Sampson handed me and shoved the receipt inside. In the end, both Pearl and I had gotten what we wanted, so there was nothing to quibble about. On top of that, we'd also discovered that Wallace Turnhill wasn't being targeted by a killer, leaving us with only one murder to solve.

Is that a bit of optimism I hear, dear hexed one?

"Good luck tomorrow," Mr. Sampson called out, with me replying in kind. No doubt, he would be rather busy with all the competitors forgetting little odds and ends.

I pushed open the door, having already braced myself for the piercing wind that was colder than Ammeline's non-beating heart. The biting weather wasn't what brought me to a dead stop before crossing the street. No, it was the faint sound of the music that I'd been hearing ever since we'd left the wharf.

Music, dear hexed one?

"Yes," I replied behind my scarf that I'd lifted to cover the lower half of my face. It took a lot for me to follow up with a plea that I already figured out would be denied. Oh, this wasn't the best way to start off our evening. We'd already established that sirens were just part of folklore, right? They simply didn't exist. "Pearl, please tell me you hear it, too."

I wish I could, Miss Lilura. Alas, I don't hear a thing. You don't suppose...

"Don't say it," I warned, hurrying across the street so

that I could drag the others outside. There was a slim chance that maybe the level of the tone prevented Pearl from hearing the melancholy sound. "There has got to be a reasonable explanation as to why you don't hear that music."

You do realize that I'm not just any average feline, correct? I'm a familiar, dear hexed one. Nothing you do or say is going to change the fact that you might actually be hearing a siren's song. It appears that Ominous Odessa no longer wishes to remain in the dark depths of the frozen lake.

Chapter Ten

"THIS IS A bad idea," Knox warned softly, always the one who was most skeptical of these types of things. He still had trouble accepting the most commonplace supernatural elements. Considering I had gone through most of my life believing that sirens were just folklore, I understood his hesitation. "We should scope out the area before blindly going into a situation that could easily have us trapped without a way out."

The situation Knox was referring to was the fact that we had returned to the inn the moment I'd informed them of what I'd been hearing all day, changing into the appropriate clothes. Basically, we had added on our snow pants for an added layer of warmth against the gusts of winds that were no doubt stronger on the lake.

That's right.

We were going out on the thick, frozen sheet of ice to search for Ominous Odessa.

I would like to point out that in my two thousand years, I have never once encountered a siren. That alone should tell you how rare they are, dear hexed one. I fear that our resident werewolf has a valid point. We have no idea what we're about to encounter, or if said happenstance is an elaborate trap.

"You mean, a trap set by Ammeline?" Piper asked, her voice merely a whisper behind the knitted facemask that she had pulled out of nowhere. She must have knitted it days ago, once she'd been made aware of what type of weather we'd be dealing with on this case. "Orwin, do you have everything we'll need?"

Orwin always came prepared with a small satchel of potions that were weapons in our arsenal. Traditional firearms wouldn't always work on the supernatural. There were wooden bullets for vampires and silver bullets for werewolves, but blessed silver ammunition wasn't always effective against other supernatural beings. We'd spent months and months searching for proper incantations and creating potions that would help defeat Ammeline should we ever be fortunate enough to discover her location or catch up to her by chance.

"All set." Orwin's words were clipped, alerting all of us to the fact that he was uneasy with the current plan. He'd managed to find goggles that fit over his glasses, and his gaze was clearly focused on the vast darkness that lay just beyond the horizon. The good thing was that the majority of the locals and tourists were at the ice-skating rink, leaving only those ice fishermen who preferred to fish at night. With them tucked away inside their shanties, it shouldn't be hard to evade detection. "I'm ready."

I wasn't so sure about that, but it wasn't like we had a choice. The feeble, alluring song was still being vocalized as we all looked out over the frozen lake. I'm sure we would have to start searching the empty shanties that were still set up, as well as the different fishing holes that had been drilled into the thick ice. The siren was calling out to me for a reason.

I worried most about Orwin, but not because we might have an encounter with a bona fide siren. You see, he was an actual descendent from Ammeline Letty Romilda. It was shocking, I know, but her blood ran in his veins. It wasn't something he liked to talk about, but he had some misplaced notion that a small part of the responsibility to stop her from doing any more damage to our kind fell on his shoulders. On the other hand, he'd coincidentally been there the day that she'd hexed me with premonitions of murder. I wasn't sold on coincidences, and the fact that Orwin had been in the right place at the right time was just a bit too much for me to accept.

Fate also has a say in the greater good, and I am a firm believer that things happen for a reason. Shall we go forth, dear hexed one?

Leave it to Pearl to be the brave one. She was a force of nature, and I didn't doubt for a second that she was on first name basis with Fate herself.

We were currently sitting on the snowmobiles, with

me and Knox on one and Orwin and Piper on the other. Pearl was invisible, though she was hitching a ride with Orwin and Piper. Typically in situations like these, she would be front and center. Unfortunately, as I'd mentioned previously, there were ice fishermen who preferred to be out at night. We'd have to maneuver around those shanties that had light streaming out from in between the wooden slats.

"Lou, you lead," Knox ordered, kicking the idling snowmobile into gear. "Orwin and Piper, stay behind us at a safe distance so you have time to react in case we come upon…whatever."

I closed my eyes behind my own goggles as Knox accelerated the snowmobile, keeping our speed as even as possible so that I could listen for the siren's call. It struck me as odd that we never once considered that Ominous Odessa actually murdered Ronald Dorsey. I figured that had to do with my vision, because folklore never once suggested that a siren could take on a human form and shove someone to their death.

No, the siren was calling out to another supernatural being for a reason. Either this was some elaborate setup by Ammeline, who had somehow figured out that we had turned the tables and were now hunting her, or the siren needed our help. She could have also simply wanted to let us know that she was innocent from any wrongdoing.

I kept my eyes closed to try and utilize only my hearing, lifting my right arm while keeping my left wrapped tightly around Knox's waist so that I wouldn't fall off the snowmobile. Knox followed my pointed finger, encased in a ski glove that also currently had a hand warmer tucked inside my palm. He changed course, allowing us to get closer to the elusive siren.

"She's taking us away from the cluster of shanties positioned to the east of us," Knox called out, somehow knowing that I wasn't using my own vision. "I don't like this, Lou."

What Knox was attempting to convey was that he didn't like the idea that only I could hear the siren. I truly didn't believe I was hearing her song for the usual reason listed in folklore—luring sailors to their death using their hypnotic songs. I'd found that I could have easily ignored the beautiful harmonics, but I was choosing not to for the sake of missing out on something bigger.

What if this was the moment we'd all been waiting for?

Over the next five minutes, Knox continued to follow my directions at a slow and methodical pace. He never stopped until I finally gave him the okay, and only then did he bring the snowmobile to a complete stop. He kept the engine idle in case we needed to make a quick getaway, but I could hear the engine from Orwin and Piper's vehicle, as well.

Nothing was as loud as the siren's song where we had

stopped, though.

"Do you seriously not hear it?" I asked, completely puzzled as to how something so loud and beautiful couldn't be heard by the others. Knox just shook his head as he lifted his goggles to get a better look at their surroundings. His eyesight was better than even Pearl's vision, given that the hex Ammeline had placed on him was being a descendant of the *Canis Lupus Occidentalis,* or better known as the McKenzie Valley variant. He was bigger, stronger, and had more of an advantage than an average werewolf. "Do you have the flashlight?"

While Knox might not have any trouble seeing in the dark, the only thing I could perceive was what was in the path of our lone headlight from the snowmobile. The siren's alluring song seemed to be coming from our right. Knox didn't reply right away as I cautiously slid off the seat, attempting to seek out the supernatural being that clearly desired something from me.

Knox followed suit, motioning for Orwin and Piper to remain on their snowmobiles. It was sweet that he wanted them to be able to take off at a moment's notice should any sign of danger be near. His inherent need to protect me had nothing to do with his curse, and everything to do with the fact that he'd served in the military. He was loyal to a fault, and we'd become part of his unit. He felt responsible.

He opened the small hatch on the back of the snow-mobile, handing me a flashlight before pointing toward the direction I'd been concentrating on. He must have seen something in the darkness. Usually, I had no trouble running headfirst into whatever awaited us. After all, I had faced down the Lich Queen. Granted, I'd come away with a few battle wounds, but I had still walked away alive.

A siren, though? Now I completely understood how Knox felt in situations like these after learning that there were indeed vampires, druids, and spirits who walked among us.

I do agree that this is quite an exhilarating moment, dear hexed one. As a matter of fact, I was having a bit of trouble reining in my curiosity that I decided to join you instead of remaining behind with my sweet Piper.

"You're just saying that because you're not the one hearing the siren's song," I whispered, turning on the flashlight and very cautiously pointing the beam in the direction that Knox was now staring at intently. He became unnaturally still when the lone ray finally rested on a rather large area, maybe six feet in circumference, that contained no ice. "Oh, my."

I realize that I sounded a lot like Pearl in this moment, but it was rare that I was speechless. In the middle of the freezing water was the most beautiful creature I'd ever set eyes on, and I wasn't exaggerating in the least. Her porcelain skin had a sheen to it from the water, yet it was almost as if she were ethereal in appearance. High cheek bones accentuated her full lips, while her blue eyes were mesmerizing. She gracefully moved her arms across the surface of the dark water as she floated in what could only be called her natural state.

Oh, my *is right, dear hexed one. This is a rare moment, indeed, and one that we must treasure.*

I sure yearned for the chance to treasure this moment in my later years, but I wasn't so sure I would be given the chance. No one else could hear her enticing song, which gave me serious pause. What were the chances that I could get away from the clutches of the supernatural underworld twice?

"I mean you no harm, hexed witch."

Oh, dear me. This particular siren seems to know who you are, Miss Lilura.

I didn't need a play by play of the situation, but maybe it was Pearl's way of remaining calm. By this time, it appeared that Orwin and Piper didn't want to miss out on the big moment, either. They were on either side of me by the time I'd taken a step farther, though Knox remained two steps ahead with his hand up, warning us not to get any closer to the alluring siren. I didn't particularly like the way her blue gaze was drawn to Knox, so I found myself replying without any thought.

"Why did you call us here?" I asked, making sure that my voice was loud enough to travel the twenty feet of ice that remained between us. I wished Knox would take a couple steps back. I didn't like him so close to the supernatural creature that could take him with her into the murky depth of the lake with just a flick of her finger. "Do you know who killed Robert Dorsey?"

Technically, the siren had only called out to me, but I hadn't been foolish enough to come alone. We all took a cautious step back in unison when the siren gracefully leaned forward to swim to the edge of the ice. She casually rested her forearms on the ledge and tilted her heart-shaped face in interest as if to gauge our intentions.

"The reason I called for you, hexed witch, is that we are bound together for eternity," she said in a rather carnal manner.

Truthfully, it was quite eerie.

I'm not particularly fond of how this creature worded that statement, Miss Lilura. I realize now isn't the best time to bring this up, but she's ruining my nickname for you.

Knox, Orwin, and Piper didn't appreciate the siren's underlying warning, either, but it had nothing to do with my nickname. Had the siren meant that our souls would be together forever in the murky depths of the lake? I had a problem with that scenario too, so I treaded cautiously so as not anger the mystifying woman.

"I don't understand," I said, being completely honest during this very awkward situation. "Are you or aren't you responsible for Ronald Dorsey's death?"

"I had nothing to do with the resident's death," the siren answered without hesitation, surprising all of us. Orwin must have taken one of the vials of potions we'd fashioned from various components around the world that weren't the easiest ingredients to obtain and tucked it in his glove. He appeared ready to throw it at the siren, but I made sure to stall him from taking such drastic action. "I called you here to discuss our connection, hexed witch."

Connection? Does this siren look familiar to you, Miss Lilura?

There was absolutely no connection between me and the siren. I didn't even doubt my answer. First, I'd never seen her before in my entire life. Second, I'd also never been to this part of Michigan. What could Ominous Odessa possibly be referring to?

"Uh-oh."

"Uh-oh?" I reiterated to Orwin with disbelief. What had he meant by that? To make matters worse, he let his arm hang down his side, meaning that he had no longer had any intention of throwing the vial toward the siren to lessen her supernatural abilities. "What does that mean?"

"You feel the connection, don't you, warlock?" the siren asked with satisfaction practically dripping from her tone. As if she were finished with these fun and games, those blue eyes that had glimmered with interest and excitement now darkened with anger. "If I thought for one second that dragging you to the depths of my home would hurt the Lich Queen, I would not hesitate to do so. Do not fear me, though. I only want to provide you with information that will help you in your hunt for the immortal wicked witch."

I once again am astounded that I can still be surprised after two thousand years roaming this earth. Don't you see, Miss Lilura? This is no ordinary siren created by simple folklore. Ammeline Letty Romilda took this witch's life and sentenced her to a lifetime of loneliness. And just when I thought things couldn't get more interesting…

Chapter Eleven

AFTER QUICKLY CATCHING Knox up on the internal conversation that Pearl and I had been having, he now understood the importance of the beautiful siren whom I still wasn't so sure we could trust. After all, these supernatural beings lured men to their death.

When you put it like that, Miss Lilura...

"I know, I know," I muttered back at Pearl, doing my best to figure out how this so-called mythical creature knew of Orwin's connection to Ammeline. Truthfully, I had a thousand questions for Odessa. "How long has it been since Ammeline cursed you to this lake?"

The timeline certainly made sense. Ammeline sought immortality in the 1700s. Ominous Odessa was first spotted in the 1800s, right when Ammeline would have been at her full power. What had the Lich Queen been doing in Michigan during that time, though? Being a psychology professor, history definitely wasn't my forte.

"All that matters are that you and your friends are hunting down the monster responsible for putting me here. It's possible that once you destroy her that I might

be released from my curse, but it's pointless to specu-
late." Odessa pushed away from the edge, seemingly not
bothered in the least that the piercing winds were enough
to make our eyes water. The cold didn't seem to affect
her at all. She once again began to gracefully tread water,
her seductive gaze landing on Knox. "You are one of a
kind, werewolf. Even you don't know your own strength.
Do the five of you really not know why you were
brought together? Familiar, show yourself. I do not like
talking to illusions."

*You need a lesson in manners, Miss Odessa. No wonder
you swim these waters alone.*

Pearl had more than chastised the siren, much to our
chagrin. She'd even given an insult to the nth degree. I
was relatively certain that we weren't in the position to
have the upper hand. Odessa had information we
needed, and she probably wouldn't be inclined to share
those details if we alienated her all because she lacked
etiquette after being cursed to swim the waters of a lake
for the past two centuries.

"In your familiar's defense, lack of etiquette might
very well be the reason I ended up in this predicament,"
Odessa shared knowingly, her blue gaze brightening with
what could only be described as humor. Her change in
mood was in complete contrast to the dark tumultuous
water surrounding her. "It is nice to have a conversation
without the hassle I usually endure from the occasional
lone ice fisherman. Back to your question, I was a witch

before this sentence was handed down to me by the Lich Queen. You see, I was one of her most dedicated acolytes. She'd been trying to create an army to take over the new supernatural territories that were being established back then, but we had soon discovered that she hadn't wanted to make peace with the settlers. Her plan was to eliminate all of them."

I reluctantly accept your half-attempt at an apology, Miss Odessa. I'll even extend myself the courtesy of guessing as to why the Lich Queen bestowed a hex on you most befitting in that insanity riddled mind of hers—you were in love with one of the humans.

Orwin was keeping Knox up on the conversation that Pearl and Odessa were having, allowing the rest of us to put together some of the puzzle that we'd been trying to construct ever since we'd begun this journey.

"I was," Odessa replied softly, the longing in her voice unmistakable. "He was beautiful, inside and out, with a heart of pure gold. He did not deserve to die just because Ammeline had foolish desires of ruling an empire, devoid of souls. I did what I had to do in order to save my love, and I do not regret the consequences. That does not mean I will not seek my revenge if the opportunity arises. And alas, here you are."

Standing still for so long in the bitter cold darkness with the gusts of winds strong enough to try and knock us back a step or two was beginning to settle in our bones. Not even the hand warmers I'd purchased earlier today could stop Piper and I from shivering as we began to understand the depth of Ammeline's depravity.

I daresay there is no limit to the Lich Queen's debauchery.

"She was clearly insane before seeking immortality," I said in abstract horror, comprehending the extent of the Lich Queen's wickedness. "We know that her soul is contained in the phylactery located on the handle of her cane, but what can you tell us that will help destroy what is left of her soul?"

"The mutual need to destroy Ammeline Letty Romilda is the reason we joined forces," Knox interrupted, seemingly focused on Odessa's previous statement. "Are you saying there was something more to us meeting? Did the Lich Queen choose us intentionally?"

"You are not only handsome, Werewolf King, but you are also very wise," Odessa replied, swimming forward once more. It was almost as if she desired to touch him, and I found myself reaching for his jacket to ensure that he couldn't be snatched away from us in the blink of an eye. "I will not take him from you, hexed witch. You will need him when the time comes."

"When the time comes for what?" I asked, afraid I already knew the answer. Something big was heading our way, and I wasn't sure any preparations could give us a leg up. "Odessa, please tell us what you know."

I wanted to scream at the siren to stop playing games and just give us the information we'd been searching for all this time. We'd been hunting Ammeline for so long that it almost seemed as if we were driving around in circles. What I didn't understand was how Odessa could even know about us if she'd been cursed to this lake for all eternity.

"Have you not guessed?" Odessa said charismatically, once again resting her forearms on the ice. I shivered for her. "I'm the first of the witches who the Lich Queen cursed after attaining her immortal form. She had never hexed someone before as a Lich, and to do so in a raging fury had consequences that I'm not even sure she is aware of to this day."

Oh, dear. I certainly did not expect this revelation, Miss Lilura. This could change everything.

"You're linked to her," Knox murmured in disbelief, grabbing my hand. We both were wearing gloves, but I could literally sense the firmness in which he gripped my fingers. "Where is she?"

There were still quite a few questions that I wanted to ask, but Knox really got straight to the point. Pearl was right when she said that this could be a game changer. We could finally get our old lives back.

And is that what you want, Miss Lilura?

"Low blow," I muttered hastily, attempting to adjust my scarf against the wind. The goggles protected my forehead, but I could no longer feel my cheeks or nose. What I could sense was my hesitation upon hearing Pearl's question, and I wasn't sure where it had come from. Knox deserved to be human again; to be able to go home to his family and resume the life he'd built after serving in the military. It wasn't fair to me either, that I'd had to leave my life behind. Why had I hesitated to answer Pearl's question then? It was something I would have to ponder at a later date, because it was doubtful that we would have much longer with Ominous Odessa. "Odessa, please share with us what you can. I can imagine that you want to be set free from your own curse. We can help you."

I am certain we shall revisit my question at another time, Miss Lilura.

"I've accepted my fate, hexed witch. I did not call you here to help me, but instead to tell you what you are up against. You see, Ammeline believes that each of you have a bigger purpose to serve in her plans...even the healer and her familiar," Odessa practically purred, much to Pearl's dismay. As a matter of fact, a few non-etiquette words might have passed her whiskers in reaction to Odessa's claim. "Listen to me closely. Ammeline Letty Romilda is preparing for an apocalypse like none other, one where she will reign as the only Lich Queen. No human or supernatural creature will stand in her way. She has waited many years and gathered numerous followers in her quest, but you five are the key to her triumph. You could also be her downfall. Unlock your roles, and only then will you stop her destruction. Good luck, travelers. You will need it."

Odessa quietly pushed off the ice until she was in the middle of the churning cold water, gradually allowing the darkness to swallow her whole. Knox and I both stepped forward, calling out her name. How could she say that Ammeline was planning some sort of apocalypse and then leave out the details? Was this some sort of game to her? Could we even believe a word she said?

You do have a point, Miss Lilura. Ominous Odessa could simply be losing what is left of her own mind after being cursed to this lake for centuries by the Lich Queen.

"That was…" Piper let her voice trail off as she had trouble coming up with the right adjective. I could relate, because I was still shell-shocked that we'd met the first witch to ever be hexed by Ammeline Letty Romilda. "I'm not sure what we just heard, but I do know that I had a choice to come with you, Lou. No one placed a curse on me or Pearl. We chose to travel with you for several reasons, and we—"

"I know that, Piper," I replied in reassurance, thinking back to when Orwin and I had purposefully sought out Piper. Orwin had spent months researching the lineage of the Allifairs to find out which witch or warlock had inherited the gift of healing. Had Ammeline known all along that we would seek the help of the Allifairs to lift the curse? It hadn't worked, of course. My affliction wasn't something natural that could be healed, and neither was Knox's hex. "Listen, there's no use staying out here in the cold. Let's head back to the inn. We can discuss what happened there, and maybe figure out this riddle that Odessa left us with. She said that we had to unlock our roles. She made it sound so easy."

"Maybe it is," Knox said grimly, turning away from the dark water. A horrible image of Odessa changing her mind and reaching out for him had me grabbing his arm and pulling him away from the black void. "But you're right, we should head back to town. The gusts of winds are only getting stronger, and we still have a murder to solve."

Our resident werewolf is handling an encounter with a sinister siren better than my sweet Piper. I'm rather impressed with his level of composure.

Orwin's sigh was loud enough that we could hear him over the small squall of flurries that were gathering to our right. We were all readjusting our goggles when Pearl's light laughter rang out, practically shattering the thick blanket of concern that had settled over us at the task of figuring out what our role was in Ammeline's plan.

"You have to agree it would have been the perfect opportunity," Orwin complained, straddling the snowmobile in frustration. "One question, followed by a simple yes or no, would have solved the UFO debate. I mean, Odessa has been in this lake for centuries. She'd know if something unexplained crashed into the water years ago and was currently lying in the deepest depth of the lake."

I have a feeling that we will be back to visit this quaint little village, alien hunter. Do not worry your little tinfoil hat over it. You will have the chance to ask your question, but are you truly prepared for the answer? I'm not sure we are ready for any of the answers that await us...

Chapter Twelve

"I DON'T LIKE this," I murmured, casting my gaze wide to include what suspects we did have left on Piper's Murder 101 app. "We should be back at the inn, going over what Odessa told us about Ammeline."

What were we doing instead? Well, I currently had a hot chocolate in my hand when what I really needed was a cup of coffee with maybe a shot of Bailey's Irish Cream for good measure. The ice rink was packed with residents and tourists alike, drawing in quite the crowd to induce excitement about tomorrow and this weekend's festivities. It was clear from the smiles, laughter, and loud conversations that these people had no idea a murderer walked or, more to the point, skated among them.

I do appreciate the spot of warm cream after being out on the frozen lake for so long, dear hexed one. I hadn't realized how cold the tips of my ears were until I'd begun to wonder if they'd fallen off. The numbness was quite unpleasant.

Piper and Orwin were skating in circles, purposefully going a bit slower than the other skaters so that he could hear their thoughts as they passed by. His plan was very strategic, and I was hoping that he'd be able to obtain some type of lead for us to close this case by sunrise.

"We won't be able to give the Ammeline situation the attention it deserves while we're on this case, so let's figure out who murdered Ronald Dorsey." Knox leaned forward on the high-top table, having allowed me take advantage of an overhead heater. The type of bitter cold that we'd endured while out on the ice this evening had caused my skin to feel as if it could shatter. I still suffered from an occasional, involuntary shiver as my body temperature slowly managed to return to normal. "Orwin was able to rule out most of our suspects. Who do we have left?"

"Well, there is still Ms. Rusco, Wallace Turnhill, and even Sheriff Torkin. You said that Orwin didn't have a chance to get close enough to Marilyn's aunt when you were in the diner earlier this evening, but I do see them on the other side of the rink." If Ms. Rusco was guilty, she was putting on a pretty good show. They'd been joined by Esther, and all three of them were currently handing out flyers to some of the tourists who'd come into town today. Most likely, they were still drumming up a crowd for the polar bear plunge. "As for Wallace, I'm not sure what his motive could be, other than that he didn't want his best friend to sell his property. Sheriff Torkin has been saying that Ronald Dorsey's death was an accident, but what if he was covering up the murder?"

I believe I'll go for a walk to see if I can hear anything that would lead us to another clue. It will give me something to do other than ponder on Ominous Odessa's riddle.

"Highly doubtful," Knox replied with a shake of his head. "Think about it. He would have had to get a lot of people on some type of dirty payroll to pull that off. The coroner's office isn't a part of the village, and they would have kept close tabs on an open investigation. Plus, Orwin was able to confirm that the coroner believed the blunt trauma found of Ronald Dorsey's head was a result of the fall into the water. They most likely assumed he hit the ice on the way down."

"I'd still like to know why George Nektar took Anne's bribe to leave town."

"Why don't we just ask?" Knox inquired, surprising me when he flashed a smile over my shoulder. Sure enough, the young woman in question was walking our way. "Follow my lead."

"Are you two having fun?" Anne asked, not as upbeat as she normally appeared. Her smile certainly didn't meet her eyes.

"Yes," Knox replied, lifting up his hot chocolate. "My sweet tooth is satisfied, though I'll leave the skating to Orwin and Piper."

Anne's red curls didn't even move as she glanced toward the rink. Something had definitely happened since we'd last saw her, and I could only guess that her mother caught onto the fact that a thousand dollars was missing from the inn's till.

"Mr. Nektar sure left in a hurry today." Knox didn't waste any time getting straight to the point. "Did you know that he was in town to scope out the area and see if any of the residents are interested in selling their land? Orwin and I rented a shanty, and Hank told us all about how a big corporation wants to come into the area and build a fancy resort. He had a few choice words to say about Mr. Nektar."

I had been expecting a couple of different responses from Anne, but her bursting into tears wasn't one of them. Knox apparently hadn't thought the conversation would end up with Anne crying, either. He quickly grabbed up some napkins and all but shoved them into her hands.

Oh, dear. Once again, I find that I can't leave you alone without trouble finding you. What have you done to this poor girl?

"I'm so sorry," Anne whispered, dabbing her eyes and glancing around to make sure that no one else had witnessed her breakdown. Her breath stuttered as she tried to compose herself. "It's just that I'm the reason he left town. I really messed up."

I retract my previous question, dear hexed one. It seems that Miss Dahl needs a confidant, and I'm glad to see that you're stepping up to the plate.

"What did you do, Anne?" I asked softly, sharing a knowing look with Knox. We had figured out from Orwin that Mr. Nektar wasn't the one responsible for

Ronald Dorsey's death, but that didn't mean he wasn't somehow connected to it. Maybe someone that he worked with had more of a hands-on approach to things. "How were you the one to cause Mr. Nektar to leave town?"

I should probably interject here that the alien hunter ruled out Mrs. Dorsey's aunt as the murderer. He and Piper skated over that way a few moments ago, so it appears that we are still at square one.

"I paid Mr. Nektar one thousand dollars in cash to leave Pikeville. I happened to overhear him talking on the phone about owing money to his brother, so I figured it was worth a shot." Anne blew her nose before she became somewhat defiant. "I was protecting this town. That man wanted to take away our homes and invade our village. I did what I thought was right. It wasn't like my mom's conversation with Ronnie had convinced him to sell, and we know that Marilyn would have caved sooner or later. She swears that's not true, but she loved that no good cheater to the very end, even though everyone knows that he was seeing Debra Lily behind Marilyn's back."

Incoming, and I'm going to guess this upcoming confrontation is going to be juicer than one of those movies that Piper streams on her computer.

"Anne Marie Dahl, how dare you say such a thing!" a woman offendedly exclaimed, having overheard everything that Anne had just confessed to us. I guessed the woman to be in her fifties, along with her identity.

Only someone accused of adultery could be that mortified. "Ronnie and I were just friends. The reason he was coming over to the house was that he wanted me to plan Marilyn's sixtieth birthday party. Shame on you for suggesting that it was anything more than that."

I daresay that Miss Dahl's freckles have disappeared.

With Anne's complexion, it was easy to tell when she was embarrassed by the fact that Debra had called her out on spreading rumors. The flush of red had not started from her neck, but instead appeared instantly and had indeed camouflaged her freckles.

"I saw the two of you, Debra Lily," Anne said defensively, especially upon realizing that people were starting to take notice of the confrontation. "You and Ronnie were dancing together in your apartment the night before he died, and it's the reason that Ominous Odessa took his life."

Needless to say, the subject of Ominous Odessa brought several other people into the conversation. Some of the residents dismissed Anne and her belief in the siren legend, while others laughed awkwardly, not quite sure what to believe. Something was nagging me though, and I couldn't figure out what it was. By this time, Orwin and Piper had skated over, though they stayed on the opposite side of the three-foot wall that separated the tables from the ice.

"...my fault, really." Henry had been standing behind Debra, shuffling his boots at the awkward conversation that was taking place. He didn't like being the center of attention, but he stood by his woman's side in solidarity. "I was the one who told Ronnie that he should finally learn the waltz. It was going to be his gift to Marilyn, along with the party."

Anne looked appropriately shamed for the direction her thoughts had taken her these past few weeks. She'd jumped to conclusions without having all of the facts, just as many of the other residents had, as well. I'd been guilty of that myself a time or two.

Miss Dahl isn't the only one who seems a bit sheepish over the rumors, dear hexed one. Take a look around.

Sure enough, there were quite a few locals who'd redirected their gazes away from Debra and Henry. They went back to their own conversations, no longer wanting to be a part of anything that might make them look just as bad as Anne for jumping to conclusions.

"We can understand how things looked to you, Anne," Henry continued, forgiveness lacing his tone. He even nodded at Debra when she didn't seem quite so willing to do the same, but the way she gave a quick nod back told us of her agreement. "We're all guilty of judging others too, at times."

I do so love a nice ending, though it would be nice to solve Mr. Dorsey's murder. Who could have been the one to hit him in the head and send him to his death?

"Did you really give that horrible man a thousand dollars to leave town?" Debra asked, letting bygones be bygones. "Henry and I both tried to talk to Ronnie about not selling his lakeside property, but he really thought Marilyn would prefer to move to Florida for their retirement. The chance to do so came earlier than expected, but I still think they would have made a mistake by going through with the sale."

"I did pay Mr. Nektar to leave town," Anne confirmed, pleased that someone agreed with the way she'd handled the situation. "I wasn't so sure that Marilyn wouldn't follow through with Ronnie's wishes. Debra, I apologize for…"

I'm sure that Ms. Dahl understood her daughter's motives, but taking a thousand dollars out of the inn's profits without telling her mother is not the way to go about things. Stealing is simply unacceptable, dear hexed one.

I caught Orwin's frown as he reacted to Pearl's sentiment, clearly something sticking out about the commentary that wasn't sitting right with him. He wasn't the only one who'd connected a puzzle piece, but I didn't want Anne or the others to notice the tension that had settled over the table. Anne, Debra, and Henry continued their conversation, allowing us to talk amongst one another.

"Did Anne say that her mother spoke with Ronald Dorsey about his plan to sell his lakeside property?" Knox asked me in such a way that I had to strain to hear every word. "I thought that Cecelia hadn't even been aware of who Mr. Nektar was until after Dorsey's death."

"Orwin?" I peered over at him, hoping that he could

help us out. I wanted to ask him if he'd ever been able to get close enough to Cecelia to pick up on her thoughts, but I was afraid that Anne would catch onto the fact that we were talking about her mother. I was closer to her, whereas Knox was on the other side of the table. "Anything?"

The alien hunter wants me to let you know that he was never in close proximity to Ms. Dahl during our stay. I don't need to say what this could mean for the young Miss Dahl.

There was only one way to know for sure if we were right, but it would require the help of Sheriff Torkin. In order for that to happen, we would need to get him to believe that Ronald Dorsey's death wasn't an accident.

Easier said than done, dear hexed one.

"Not necessarily," Orwin muttered, pulling on Piper's hand so that they began to skate away. He called out over his shoulder, not worried about who would hear him now. "Lou and Knox, meet us back at the inn."

That was the alien hunter's way of telling you and our resident werewolf that there is a plan in place. I sure hope it's a good one too, because the clock is ticking on that upcoming dip in the freezing lake tomorrow morning. It's times like these that I love being a beautiful regal feline.

Chapter Thirteen

"ANNE MARIE DAHL, you're under arrest for theft," Sheriff Torkin announced, his voice grim while the deep frown on his face spoke volumes. "You have the right to remain silent..."

When the alien hunter puts his mind to something, he certainly doesn't disappoint.

While the sheriff continued to read Anne her rights in the main room of the inn, the rest of us stood near the massive hearth in shock at the way Orwin's plan was being carried out. We'd known it would involve Sheriff Torkin, because he was the one who needed to be convinced that Ronald Dorsey's death wasn't an accident. What we hadn't guessed was the specific drastic measure that had been chosen, because arresting Anne hadn't even crossed my mind.

"You're no longer the innocent young man who was standing on campus the day I was hexed, are you?" I muttered in disbelief as Anne began to cry as the sheriff placed the cold metal cuffs around her wrists. I rested a hand over my heart. "I'm so proud."

My comment did illicit a bark of laughter covered up by a cough from Knox, although Piper looked to be anything but impressed. From the glares she was shooting at Orwin, I'm pretty sure he would have been able to figure out if there was UFO at the bottom of the lake without any help from Ominous Odessa.

My sweet Piper, I'll admit that the alien hunter's plan is a bit unorthodox. While a bit merciless, this particular strategy should indeed lure a confession from Ms. Dahl. No matter what her intentions were when she went out on the ice to speak with Mr. Dorsey, a crime was still committed. Murder is murder, after all.

"Cecelia won't allow her daughter to be arrested," Orwin confirmed as we continued to observe the scene before us. Cecelia had hurried out of the office, all but ordering the sheriff to stay away from her daughter. Anne, by this point, was a blubbering mess. I didn't blame her, really, but there was an underlying callous layer to her mother that couldn't be allowed to continue should someone else venture into town with an offer from Mr. Nektar's company. "At least, that's my hope."

"How did you convince the sheriff that Ronald Dorsey was murdered?" Knox asked, using the arm of the couch to lean back against as we all stood on the area rug as a collective group to watch the show unfold. "It couldn't have been easy."

"Well, I might have embellished Anne's meeting with George Nektar," Orwin admitted, sliding a wary glance at Piper. He was clearly worried that she wouldn't forgive him for utilizing Anne in this trap. "The sheriff believes that both were in on the murder, but I'm sure Cecelia will clear up any misunderstandings."

You have faith in a mother's love, alien hunter. I'm impressed with your creative strategy. So much so that I will give you two free questions about my knowledge of the JFK assassination. After that, my whiskers are knotted.

How Orwin didn't rub his hands together in glee was beyond me, but Cecelia was now changing tactics. The sheriff had convinced her that new information had come to light about Ronald Dorsey's death. He explained that he was going to take Anne in for questioning based on the payment she gave George Nektar, as well as where she'd been on the night of Mr. Dorsey's murder. Cecelia basically tried everything to get the sheriff to release Anne, but he wasn't faltering in his duty. There was only one thing left for her to do if she wanted to spare Anne the humiliation of being dragged down to the station, and that was confess to the crime.

"Sheriff, wait," Cecelia ordered sharply, taking him aback. She gritted her teeth in what could only be called cold fury. She wasn't a sweet, innocent neighbor, after all. There was a ruthless businesswoman behind that pert nose and dusting of freckles that would have fooled anyone into believing that she only had good intentions. "Anne did nothing wrong. I gave her that money to get rid of George Nektar. There isn't anything wrong with paying someone to leave town that I know of, especially if he was willing to take the money."

"This isn't just about the money, Cecelia." Sheriff Torkin kept one hand wrapped around Anne's upper left arm as he leveled her mother a stare. "New information has come to light that Ronnie's death wasn't an accident. We're reopening the investigation, and I'm bringing in the state police. They have better forensics than the county, and I'm almost certain they're going to find evidence that Ronnie was murdered. Were the two of you in on it together?"

"We all know that Ominous Odessa was the one who took Ronnie's soul," Anne cried out, using her right shoulder to wipe the tears from her right cheek. We all tensed when she brought up the old legend that wasn't an old wives' tale, after all. "She's real. I saw her with my own eyes when I was little."

"Anne, don't you dare say another word about that foolish myth," Cecelia warned, clearly weighing her options. We were all banking on the fact that Cecelia wouldn't let her daughter take the fall for murder, but who knew how far she would go to get away with killing a man. "Sheriff, all you have is that we paid Mr. Nektar to leave town. You can't tell me that you want to see this town sold off into bits and pieces until there is nothing left to call home."

"Ronnie was my friend, Cecelia," Sheriff Torkin replied with grief and anger. He didn't wear the badge solely because it was his job. It was clear that he loved this town just as much as Cecelia, but he stood in the name of justice. "As I said, we're launching a full investigation. The state police should be here within the hour. Let's go."

I do so respect the sheriff's resolve in this matter. I'm glad to see him stepping up to the plate.

The sheriff didn't even get to turn Anne toward the door when Cecelia stepped forward, clearly losing a bit of her composure. There was a mixture of panic and fury written on her features, and my intuition told me that it wouldn't be long before she confessed to murder in order to save her daughter.

"I was the one who hit Ronnie on the head," Cecelia finally declared, still no sense of shame in her assertion. "Anne had no part in this, so you can release her this instant."

"Mom, why would you say something like that?" Anne asked, her tears now dry as shock began to settle in. "You would never…"

"I would do whatever was necessary to keep this town whole," Cecelia stated defiantly as she straightened her shoulders. "Sheriff, release my daughter. You can take me down to the station, but I expect my one phone call. It was an accident, after all. I simply lashed out at Ronnie after he told me to get out of his shanty. It hadn't been my intention to hurt him. I must have had a moment of temporary insanity, wouldn't you say?"

I would say that I'm shocked at the cunningness Ms.

Dahl is exhibiting, but I do believe I'm just grateful that none of us happened to get on her bad side during our stay.

It took a few moments for Cecelia to convince the sheriff that Anne had nothing to do with Ronald Dorsey's murder. Still, he requested that the young woman come down to the station to give her statement to the state police detective, who was no doubt already on his way to town. The sheriff promised to give a woman by the name of Gwen a call to come and help out with the guests while Anne was busy at the station, a roundabout way of saying that Cecelia wouldn't be returning to the inn anytime soon.

"Gwen is one of the employees who takes care of the rooms," Orwin explained once we'd reclaimed our seats next to the fireplace. "I feel bad for Anne. Can you imagine having a murderer for a—"

Orwin cut off his words midsentence when he realized where he was going with that sentiment. Ammeline Letty Romilda was a distant relative of his, so he understood exactly how Anne would react to having the same blood running through her veins as someone capable of murder. Who knew that there could be a sliding scale for multiple layers of evil, though? Murder versus the apocalypse. Both were unacceptable. Piper patted his arm in sympathy, though she kept a close eye on our surroundings.

Cecelia's arrest had drawn quite the crowd, and the lobby was now full of guests who hadn't wanted to miss all the excitement. Pearl needed to remain invisible, but we'd be calling it a night soon. We would be able to leave at dawn, thus avoiding emerging ourselves into freezing water. I'd make sure to leave a hefty donation for the animal shelter, though.

That's very kind of you, dear hexed one. Maybe Ms. Esther will buy that goat of hers a pen so that he doesn't continue to harass her guests.

"We'll leave first thing in the morning," I said quietly, having taken the overstuffed chair closest to the hearth. The heat was much needed after spending so much time out on the ice, though the cold weather wasn't the reason I couldn't stop the chills from running down my spine. "I'd like to be gone before dawn breaks."

"We need to talk about what happened tonight." Knox's statement wasn't unexpected, but this was the wrong time and place. There were too many people around, and it might also be beneficial to let the information we'd gathered tonight sink in. "There's a bigger scheme at work here, and I don't like being in the dark."

"Now that we know where it all started, I can do some research," Orwin proposed, mindful of his words. It wouldn't do to be overheard talking about witchcraft and immortality. "It will take time, but at least we're no longer shooting in the dark."

"I can ask my parents to send me the old journals from my grandfather's side of the family," Piper offered, though we all knew that she wasn't referring to journals. The healers in her family had kept detailed grimoires throughout the generations. There could very well be something inside one of them that referenced the Lich Queen and her immortality. "We'll need to pick a town and rent a post office box."

Pearl was being uncharacteristically quiet. The fact that she wasn't interjecting her witticism set me on edge, and I was already teetering on the ledge. I didn't need much of a push to send me over.

"My run-in with Ammeline wasn't accidental." Knox appeared to want to say more, but he thought better of it. He was standing with his back to the fire, so he must be suffocating even without his jacket. His need to survey his surroundings was paramount, though. He was a warrior through and through. Was that why Ammeline had chosen him? "Orwin, is there a way we can run a search on my ancestors without going through one of those public databases?"

"Yes," Orwin replied, keeping things simple. We'd talk in more detail when we were back in our traveling home. The RV had become a sanctuary, of sorts. It might actually be a good idea to drive to the campsite tonight. "I can do that."

"Pearl?" I murmured, wary of the fact that she had still yet to add in her two cents. "Talk to us."

Did you know that Egyptian religion saw that death by snakebite would secure one's immortality, Miss Lilura? My dearest Cleopatra truly believed in such things, and I'm beginning to wonder if me being chosen by my sweet Piper to be her familiar wasn't due to the hands of Fate. It appears that our alien hunter has his work cut out for him.

Knox leaned down so that I could whisper to him

what Pearl had theorized, but the truth was that we weren't sure of anything. We'd solved one mystery, only to be given a bigger one.

We have solved another mystery, haven't we? Do you know what that tells me, dear colleagues? It shows me that we can do anything that we set our minds to, and that includes stopping a supernatural apocalypse.

"Uh-oh," Piper chimed in, knowing exactly what direction Pearl was headed in with her uplifting speech. She filled Knox in on what was about to happen. "This one ought to be a doozy."

For a brief moment, everything was right again. Orwin pushed up his black-rimmed glasses with a smile, Pearl's blue eyes were twinkling with humor, and Knox stood by as our silent protector as we'd gathered together. I thought back to my hesitation on bringing this hunt to an end, and I recognized the reason why— these four individuals had become my family in many ways. I wasn't ready for us to go our separate ways, so I sat back to secretly enjoy the bad joke that Pearl was about to share with us.

Knock-knock.

"Who's there?" we all asked in unison.

Armageddon.

"Armageddon who?"

Armageddon cold out there!

~ THE END ~

Thank you for helping solve yet another murder mystery with Lou and the gang! Their pursuit of Ammeline Letty Romilda is far from over, so keep an eye out for more stories in the Hex on Me Mysteries! In the meantime, and if you haven't already, feel free to dive into the Paramour Bay Mysteries…

kennedylayne.com/magical-blend.html

USA Today Bestselling Author Kennedy Layne switches creative gears and brings you a cozy paranormal mystery that will have you wishing these unique and comical characters could spring to life with a twitch of your nose…

An inherited tea shop, a quaint little Connecticut town, and its quirky residents have Raven Marigold believing her luck is about to change for the better. Of course, that was before she and her best friend found a dead body in the back of the charming store. Things go from bad to worse when Raven begins to hear a talking cat spouting on and on about magic and mayhem.

Once Raven accepts that she's not losing her mind, she finds herself in the middle of a murder investigation while discovering her family's unusual lineage—the Marigolds are bona fide witches!

'Tis the season to be scared and delighted…this wickedly charming tale includes magical tea blends, an enchanting spell book, and an eerie cottage on the edge of town that contains a special surprise you won't want to miss!

BOOKS BY KENNEDY LAYNE

THE WIDOW TAKER TRILOGY
The Forgotten Widow
The Isolated Widow
The Reclusive Widow

HEX ON ME MYSTERIES
If the Curse Fits
Cursing up the Wrong Tree
The Squeaky Ghost Gets the Curse
The Curse that Bites
Curse Me Under the Mistletoe
Gone Cursing

PARAMOUR BAY MYSTERIES
Magical Blend
Bewitching Blend
Enchanting Blend
Haunting Blend
Charming Blend
Spellbinding Blend
Cryptic Blend
Broomstick Blend
Spirited Blend
Yuletide Blend
Baffling Blend

ABOUT THE AUTHOR

First and foremost, I love life. I love that I'm a wife, mother, daughter, sister… and a writer.

I am one of the lucky women in this world who gets to do what makes them happy. As long as I have a cup of coffee (maybe two or three) and my laptop, the stories evolve themselves and I try to do them justice. I draw my inspiration from a retired Marine Master Sergeant that swept me off of my feet and has drawn me into a world that fulfills all of my deepest and darkest desires. Erotic romance, military men, intrigue, with a little bit of kinky chili pepper (his recipe), fill my head and there is nothing more satisfying than making the hero and heroine fulfill their destinies.

Thank you for having joined me on their journeys…

Email: kennedylayneauthor@gmail.com

Facebook: facebook.com/kennedy.layne.94

Twitter: twitter.com/KennedyL_Author

Website: www.kennedylayne.com

Newsletter:
www.kennedylayne.com/meet-kennedy.html